MAGICAL MAYA

MAGICAL MAYA

Adventures of Bobby and Eli

Nick Cherukuri

iUniverse, Inc.
Bloomington

Magical Maya
Adventures of Bobby and Eli

iUniverse books may be ordered through booksellers or by contacting:

iUniverse
1663 Liberty Drive
Bloomington, IN 47403
www.iuniverse.com
1-800-Authors (1-800-288-4677)

ISBN: 978-1-4620-0876-6 (sc)
ISBN: 978-1-4620-0877-3 (dj)
ISBN: 978-1-4620-0878-0 (ebk)

Library of Congress Control Number: 2011906663

Printed in the United States of America

iUniverse rev. date: 05/19/2011

PROLOGUE

1527 A.D.

The sky grew dark quickly. Weapon-clad forces arose from either side of the plain, taunting each other and waving long obsidian spears. Priests chanted incantations and analyzed the astrological signs. Medics erected makeshift hospitals to tend to the inevitable influx of the wounded. All precautions were being taken.

A dark, muscular man emerged from the advancing crowd and cried out,

"Topiltzin, you have wronged the Toltecs. Now you must feel their anger!"

The Toltecs leapt up and down at their leader's words. The air over the battleground filled with tension as the roar of the crowd increased. The battle was nearing.

On the opposing field, the Mayan king yelled back in challenge.

"Hurukan, the Mayans are peaceful people. But now for your insult and treachery, you will pay!"

The Toltec king, Hurukan, bellowed, "Fools. We now have an ally only God can destroy!"

With a roar, King Hurukan raised his red chert[1] sword and thrust it towards the Mayans.

Trumpets blared and both forces crashed into each other as the sun set, a blood-red sun.

---

1 Type of metal used

CHAPTER ONE

2010 A.D.

Bobby woke with a pang between his eyes.

"Eli!" he cried out. "Stop playing with my glasses!"

His brother handed the glasses back and slowly ten-year-old Eli Irukurehc came into focus.

"Okay, okay, can't you take a joke?" grumbled Eli. "I hate being the only fourth-grader in this camp."

As Eli stomped off towards his sleeping bag, Bobby stared at him. It wasn't that Bobby didn't like his younger brother; it was just that Bobby's life was not as exciting as he wanted it to be. It seemed as if his entire life had been planned for him, from his going to Andover Prep, to Andover, eventually to Harvard and then becoming a notable lawyer. The Irukurehcs were one of the most respected families in Boston. His great-grandpa, Aleksandar, escaped the Nazis as a youth in Macedonia and received a government grant to study at Harvard. After Aleksandar graduated, he established Irukurehc and Associates, an archeological company. The rest was history. By teaming up with the leading investors of his day, Aleksandar transformed Irukurehc & Associates into a first-class archaeological firm that handled work all over the globe. And so the stage was set. Every member of the Irukurehc family had to live up to Aleksandar's reputation and uphold the family name.

But it seemed to Bobby that nothing interesting ever happened to him, that he was a programmed robot.

But a programmed robot that longed to malfunction!

That was why he had decided to accompany his parents to the Mayan archeological campsite in Chich'en Itzá, Mexico. He had never been on such a trip, so he thought why not try something new? He also had a school assignment on Mayan life, and some hands-on experience would be the best type of preparation. All the people in his family were dedicated scientists who never kidded about anything and took everything way too seriously. Although Bobby appreciated all the knowledge that flowed in the family, it did grow heavy sometimes.

Fortunately, Eli always spiced things up with his infamous antics, which earned him the name of "The Elimeister" in school. Sometimes he wondered how Eli was part of the family in the first place.

Major Maya sites of the Classic and Post-Classic periods.

"Whoa! Look how far we've travelled!" Eli spoke quietly to himself.

Bobby looked at his brother. Eli was always fascinated with history and geography and could bore anyone to death by asking them to quiz him about his voluminous knowledge of those subjects. He could name any capital of any country. His favorite toy was a small portable globe that his parents had bought him. It was a clever ploy on his parents' part to silence Eli's constant chatter by keeping him occupied with the globe while they travelled.

Right now, Eli was running his little round pinky finger over the globe, tracing the route they had followed. His golden brown hair fell over his forehead, covering his equally round, chubby face, which was a product of spending the majority of the summer at McDonald's for lunch. Everyone said that Eli looked like Bobby which the older brother could hardly understand. While Eli was shorter, pudgier and tanned, Bobby was tall, lanky and extremely pale. Each of the brother's personalities further accentuated the difference.

"We started here--in Boston, Massachusetts--America. We travelled a looong way down south, past the Gulf of Mexico and reached the Yucatan peninsula in Mexico," said Eli excitedly. "Wow."

He continued tracing the globe, turning it around slowly, saying, "To the east is Cuba and to the south are Belize and Guatemala. But we're still on the continent of North America."

"Bobby, do you know that Guatemala is a beautiful country? It's tropical cause it's mostly made up of rainforests."

Bobby finished brushing his teeth and began changing into his travelling clothes. He was pretty sure that there was a trip planned today and wanted to dress appropriately.

"Hey Eli! Remember—I went to Guatemala with my Boy Scout group? Our scouts, and our local church, go there every year to help with medical clinics." he said, stretching.

Eli was still preoccupied in his own world of global finger trotting.

"Ahh!..I wish I could go to Guatemala some day!" sighed Eli, dropping his head backward with a wistful look on his face.

Bobby laughed. "Yeah! You wish you could visit *every* place on this planet. You're here in Mexico and visiting Chich'en Itzá, just hours away from Cancun, paradise of the beach resort world!"

It was true. After their stay in Chich'en Itzá for the next week, they were heading to Cancun to stay at the Barcelo Maya Hotel.

His blissful thoughts of warm beaches and palm trees were interrupted by a loud voice that wafted toward their tent.

"Bobby, unless you don't want to eat any breakfast, you'd better come here now!" cried Ms. Fletcher, the tour guide.

Being the only two kids at the campsite was a serious drawback since all the adults' focus was on you. Even the tent the brothers were assigned to was in the center, surrounded by other larger tents for the adults. Bobby put on his gold watch, quickly reached for his notebook and ran outside to the fire. He wasn't sure if the bread and slice of bacon he had just grabbed from the simmering grill would be enough to keep him hiking for the three miles to Chich'en Itzá, but it would be better than nothing. He seized Eli's hand and trudged down the trail path to catch up with the adults.

CHAPTER TWO

Chich'en Itzá - El_Castillo: In 2007, El Castillo was named one of the New Seven Wonders of the World after a worldwide vote. Picture shows El Castillo during EQUINOX day - Zigzag shadow of a rattlesnake that slithers down to the serpent's head at the base.

"Welcome to Chich'en Itzá!" said Ms. Fletcher. "Please take some time to enjoy these views from the foot of the Pyramid!

"We'll meet back here in half an hour to go over some information about this site." Ms. Fletcher was a stout, middle-aged woman. Her energetic face was sheltered from the sun by a large straw cap.

The group dispersed, some walking towards the ruins of the palace while others simply stared at the looming Pyramid of Quetzalcoatl, known as the Pyramid of Kukulcan by the ancient Mayans and as El Castillo by the Spanish.

Bobby could barely believe his eyes. He had seen pictures of Chich'en Itzá and heard about the Pyramid of Quetzalcoatl's recent inclusion into the Seven Wonders of the World, but it was something different to actually see the place with his own eyes. Being an avid reader, he held a deep fascination for ancient kingdoms, royal kings, and their warfare. He had read about the Mayans and their mysterious disappearance.

On this day, standing at the foot of the Pyramid of Quetzalcoatl, he was awestruck by the aging beauty.

"What symmetry!" he thought, looking at the square-based, stepped pyramid. Bobby was an Honor student in math and his mind started imagining how the structure had been built so perfectly when there were no sophisticated physical tools, and no computer programs such as AUTOCAD or MICROSTATION to create the needed drawings. How the Mayans had built such a magnificent structure was a nod to their unrivalled engineering abilities.

Likewise Eli, who normally did not care much about architectural things, stood beside his brother with his mouth hanging open in awe. Bobby could guess how his brother must be feeling. After all, Eli still had trouble drawing a straight line.

Before the pair knew it, half an hour had passed and they went back to join their group that was around Ms. Fletcher.

"You are at the site of the ancient capital of the Mayan Empire— Chich'en Itzá, founded in 514 A.D. These stone buildings were built with such sound architecture that they remain largely intact even after thousands of years of wear and tear." said Ms. Fletcher, spreading out her arms widely, as she walked backwards, facing her audience.

Bobby always wondered how tour guides walked with such ease in a backward motion; maybe it was one of the qualities they had to be checked for to apply for the job.

"Walk backward now—twenty-five, twenty-four...three, two, and finally one! Great—you've got excellent back-walking skills—the job is yours." His mind pictured a sample interview process.

"I am sure you appreciate the extraordinary skill and craftsmanship unique to the Mayans." Ms. Fletcher's voice, and a gentle nudge from his mother, brought the boy's attention back to the pyramid.

"The Mayans were a major Mesoamerican civilization in the pre-Columbian Americas, noted, among their many other achievements, as the only civilization in the region to have developed a written language," she continued, pointing to the inscriptions on the stone walls.

"What is Mesoamerican? It's not Native American, is it?" Eli asked loudly, and then, true to his appetite for food, whispered in Bobby's ear, "Sounds like Miso soup to me."

"Well—it means Middle America; it refers to the cultural area in the Americas, extending approximately from central Mexico to Honduras and Nicaragua.

"The culture first appeared during the pre-Classic period around 2000 B.C.E. and dissolved as an empire sometime around 1000 A.D. However the Mayans remained as a major people, divided into kingdoms, until the arrival of the Spaniards. Mysteriously, they abandoned their own exquisite cities, and let the forests take over these structures!"

She paused, taking a sip from her water bottle.

"What made the Mayans leave their cities with all these extraordinary buildings they constructed? That is still a mystery!"

"Was it a drought or famine?" someone from the crowd asked.

"Good point! That is indeed one of the theories. However, there are many others too, such as desertion or even war."

The group was silent for a moment. Why did the Mayans abandon their cities?

"O.K.—now back to the Pyramid and its unique features! Let's assemble under the shade here," continued Ms. Fletcher, moving towards the area where the pyramid cast its shadow under the blazing sun.

"The Pyramid of Kukulcan is a poetic combination of the Mayans' main passions: religion, philosophy, astronomy, and architecture. They were able to create a spectacular sight of contrasting light and shadow, twice a year, during the Spring Equinox and the Autumn Solstice," she said, pointing toward the Pyramid.

"Yeah—I can't imagine how this spectacle was better than our Super Bowl! Nothing can beat that!" muttered Eli. Bobby gave him an annoyed look, and motioned with his hand for him to listen.

"Only on these two days, the shine of the sun produces true magic! As you can see, the pyramid has four sides. But this spectacle only occurs on the steps on the north side—the Northern Staircase. Let's walk to that side."

The group excitedly followed her.

"Okay—here we are! On this northern side of the pyramid, the sun casts a zigzag shadow, forming a splendid image of a rattlesnake. Alternating triangles of bright light and dark shadow stretch from the top of the pyramid to the bottom where the light finally connects perfectly with the carved stone snake's head at the foot of the pyramid. What needs to be appreciated here is the Mayans' careful observation of the sun's movement, and their accurate positioning of the temple. As we know, the Mayans deeply worshiped the Sun as well as serpents. Serpents and the Sun are also depicted in many of their stone carvings. In this case, they captured both of them!

"Not all visitors have the good fortune of seeing this image as it occurs only on two days: the Spring Equinox and the Autumn Solstice."

Ms. Fletcher continued with her unending flow of information. She seemed very comfortable in the hot surroundings, with her large straw hat, cooling glasses, and a light yellow, open necked cotton top. Bobby's mother had told them that they were very lucky to have Sarah Fletcher as their guide. She was originally from America and had researched the Mayan Civilization for her Ph.D. at Harvard. Normally, she did archeological digs by herself, but had decided this year to accompany Irukurehc and Associates. She was one of the leading experts on the Mayans and had a genuine interest in the culture.

"See—this is an example of pure dedication to one's interests. You can tell she really enjoys being immersed in these surroundings and spreading knowledge," Mom had told them.

Mom never lets a chance go by to not highlight the importance of education and knowledge, thought Bobby, with a smile on his face. He continued listening to Ms. Fletcher.

"The Mayans were some of the most advanced scientists of their time and even had a 365-day calendar. There are 91 steps on each of the four sides of the pyramid, which lead to the shared temple platform at the top. Anyone see the connection?" Ms. Fletcher asked, with her hand on her hip.

Bobby did a quick calculation and shouted from the back, "Four times 91 equals 364, plus the shared step at the top gives 365—the number of days in a year!"

"Someone's paying attention." Ms. Fletcher smiled. Eli rolled his eyes.

"This pyramid was built to honor their main god Kukulcan, the feathered serpent, around the twelfth century A.D. Located inside the pyramid are the famous Chac Mool sculpture and the Jaguar Throne."

MAYA CHAC MOOL. The Chac-Mool depicts a human figure in a position of reclining with the head up and turned to one side, usually holding a tray over the stomach. The meaning of the position or the statue itself remains unknown.

"Wow! Throne! I'd like to sit on it—I AM THE KING! HERE COMES THE KING," Eli squealed in excitement, dramatizing his voice and walk, and placing his hands on his head, as if wearing a heavy crown.

"Unfortunately, visitors are not allowed inside the pyramid, as several precious stones and pieces of jewelry have been burglarized from the sculptures," said Ms. Fletcher, pouring cold water on Eli's enthusiasm.

Bobby looked around at several other buildings that he had heard about.

The majestic observatory where the Mayans had observed the stars long before any other Mesoamerican civilization; the Sacred Cenote where sacrifices and royal ascendance were determined.

JAGUAR THRONE. Kukulcan's Jaguar Throne, interior temple of "El Castillo". It is no longer on display, after the teeth and eyes were stolen by visitors.

But where were the famous Ulama courts?

"Anyone interested in games would like to see this—follow me!" said Ms. Fletcher, as if reading Bobby's mind. She took the group over to the great Ball Court.

"This court is 168 meters in length and 70 meters wide— home to the oldest and most popular ball game in Mesoamerica, Ulama. Ulama is a game in which two teams try to kick a heavy rubber ball through hoops positioned high on parallel walls," she said, pointing to stone hoops on the walls of the ball court.

"Ulama was such an intense game that the losing team was sometimes sacrificed to the gods!" Several people exclaimed upon hearing this.

Someone asked for Ms. Fletcher to show how the Mayans kicked the ball into the hoops. The tubby lady tried, producing extremely comical results. Bobby turned to smile at Eli, only to find his brother about fifty feet away, gazing at a small pond.

Chich'en Itzá – Ball Court View. It is the largest ball court in ancient Mesoamerica. The sides of the interior of the ball court are lined with sculpted panels depicting teams of ball players, with the captain of the losing team being decapitated.

"Eli, stop looking at the fish and come back here!"

His younger brother ran back throwing him a dirty look.

"What? I forgot to go to the bathroom at the campsite!"

Sometimes Bobby wondered why taking care of Eli wasn't a full-time job.

The brothers walked back to the group where Ms. Fletcher was explaining using her arms to emphasize her point.

"These structures represent the Mayans' past greatness for the world to see. The Mayans had advanced medical procedures too."

However, what the Mayans' medical procedures were, Bobby never heard because at that moment Eli elbowed him in the stomach and said, "Come on, let's get out of here. I think I know a shortcut back. This lecture is about as interesting as Mr. Exeter's math class."

Bobby stood for a moment, but the thought of a warm campfire and an early meal was too much for him to resist. Both his parents were still listening attentively to Ms. Fletcher's explanations. Like any true Irukurehc they were completely engrossed.

Farewell! Chich'en Itzá! Bobby looked longingly at the pyramid one last time, and jogged after his brother into the thick forest. Little did he know that it would not be his last time at the site.

CHAPTER THREE

Hours later, a steady, comforting atmosphere reigned over the campsite. Having finished their grilled burgers, Bobby and Eli were relaxing in their tent and leisurely chatting.

"I'm telling you, Bobby, the Red Sox are going to crush the Yankees this season with Matsuzaka and Pedroia," said an unusually drowsy Eli as he lay on his makeshift bed. "I'm just waiting to quiet those crazy New York fans this year."

"Yeah, you wish!"

Eli, an ardent Red Sox fan, always talked as if his team was going to win every game they played. Bobby pulled out his backpack to get some food.

"You want any chips? Mr. Ambani gave some to me for helping him clean up the pit."

The pit was a hole in the ground into which the group threw all their trash. It had to be emptied every day unless they wanted rats or, worse, jaguars to come visit at night.

"Sure, thanks," said Eli. "By the way, did Dad get angry when he found out that we ditched Ms. Fletcher's lecture?"

After a couple of minutes, Eli realized that for some reason his brother was not answering his question.

"Bobby, Bobby, you there?"

However, Bobby was looking worriedly at his left arm and frantically checking his pockets. At last, he whispered nervously, "Eli, you know that watch I had for a long time, you know, the one Grandpa gave me before he died?"

"Yeah," said Eli, "So what about it?"

"Well...I think I lost it. I can't seem to find it anywhere," said Bobby. He hurriedly added, "But don't tell anyone yet because Mom's going to kill me if she finds out."

"What! You think you lost it? Where on earth do you think it happened?" said Eli, his voice rising.

"I don't know, but just calm down for a moment, all right? I think that it's by the giant stone pyramid in Chich'en Itzá--I loosened it a bit because it was so hot, and then, you know, when I was running after you, it might have fallen off."

"Yeah, yeah—you always find a way to blame everything on me," said Eli, lowering his voice somberly, in understanding of the dire situation.

"I only noticed it just now, and we were here all afternoon," said Bobby, unhappily.

"So that's why you had that look on your face. And here I was thinking that the double cheeseburger you ate caused you diarrhea or something like that."

Bobby indeed had a very troubled look on his face.

"I might as well go tell Mom and Dad what happened tonight," he said gloomily. "By the time we go back tomorrow, the watch will be long gone. You know how many people go to Chich'en Itzá each day." He sat at the edge of his camp bed, bending forward and rubbing his hands together anxiously. "She'll be really upset hearing this!"

Bobby knew all too well what the watch meant not only to his Mom, but also to her entire family. The watch was presented to the boys' grandfather, Nura, as a wedding gift by their great—grandfather, Aleksandar himself. It was a vintage 1942 Rolex watch made of stainless steel and fourteen karat gold. It had cost over a thousand dollars back then and was priceless today. It was the only family item that Aleksandar had been able to bring with him as he fled the Nazis. Knowing its history, Nura took such good care of it, with not a single scratch after wearing it every day until he died. Not everyone had a watch in those days; most people approximated the time by watching the movement of the sun. The brothers' mother used to tell them.

"Bobby, Eli—see how carefully Grandpa has used this watch– it could be easily mistaken for a new watch." She would motion them to come over and examine it each time they were in Grandpa's presence.

Their grandpa, sitting in his rocking chair on the back porch, would turn the watch around his wrist gently, with a proud grin on his aging, wrinkled face. Like Aleksandar, Nura came from a farming background, and was the first in his family to have earned a college degree. He was revered by his children, siblings and grandchildren. Everyone looked up to him for sound advice.

One summer, when the entire family was together, in the midst of all of their uncles, aunts and cousins, his grandpa bestowed the watch on Bobby.

"After I pass away, I want to give the watch to Bobby—my oldest grandson," he declared. Looking at the amazed boy straight in the eye, he affirmed, "You are destined for great things, my boy. Always remember that. Anyone who has ever used this watch has been destined for greatness."

Bobby's mom quickly wiped away tears of joy upon hearing his words. She was very close to her father, and this meant a lot to her.

Knowing the history of the watch, Bobby felt a sense of pride, yet at the same time he felt overwhelmed by the thought of being the bearer of a family treasure. He pictured every relative of his grabbing his arm, and turning it to examine the condition of the watch each time they met. He felt scared at the thought of fat uncle Smoky, with his huge puffing pipe in his mouth, cracking his arm around to study the watch carefully. The thought made him shudder. But above all, he was happy about the confidence his Grandpa had in him.

Bobby was old enough to remember when Grandpa died. From that day on, he promised himself that he would take care of the watch like his most prized possession. And he certainly had taken really good care of it ever since. The entire household was proud of Bobby's handling of it, and he aced each and every inspection test.

Until today! He sighed in resignation.

"Well, this has certainly ruined the trip." He waited for his brother to say something. But there was only silence.

"Eli?"

Bobby glanced at his brother—he was sitting on the corner of his bed with a strange gleam in his eye.

"Are you okay?" he asked, "Or did those refried beans give you the burps too?"

"Bobby, what if we go back today?" asked Eli, who clearly had not heard what his brother had just said.

"Okay, those beans clearly affected your brain! Chich'en Itzá's been closed for hours now, and how can we go with our parents probably sleeping?"

"No, you misunderstood me. What I'm talking about is going back there tonight...at midnight! No one will find out!" whispered Eli. He had an excited look on his face.

"Are you crazy? Do you know how many things could happen? We could be caught and be sent to juvenile jail! Then what would our parents say? And we don't even know what's out there; if some animal gets us, nobody for miles can come and help us!"

"Fine! Complain now and face Mom's wrath later. You know how much that watch means to all of us. *Especially* to her!" Eli raised his voice, as if delivering an ultimatum. "Anyway, we're going out there for a legitimate reason, finding a lost personal item that holds a lot of emotional baggage. If someone finds us, we can act like two innocent children who got lost. Imagine what Barry and Tim would say back at school!"

Barry Changett and Tim Zaparex were two neighborhood friends of theirs back in Boston.

"I would go if I were you," Eli prompted, sensing Bobby's hesitation.

Bobby put his clothes back in his trunk and started to clear his bed. Listening to Eli never led to good outcomes as he had regrettably learned from past experiences. Once, Eli had persuaded him to throw paper airplanes at his Latin teacher while she was writing on the board, in retribution for the teacher's having failed him. Bobby had gotten an "A" in all subjects, except in Latin, and he took it pretty hard.

"Do it! You'll get your revenge and it'll be funny," said Eli. A bad paper airplane throw later, Bobby found himself sitting in the principal's office with a really angry Latin teacher.

But sometimes the call for action overcame the huge potential downside. Besides, he wasn't exactly looking forward to the confrontation with his parents and the inevitable consequences. He looked over at his brother who was now lying on his front, swinging his legs together in the air, and reading a book about ancient Mayan warfare with his flashlight. He studied Eli for a minute. After all, every time the pair got into trouble, Eli would somehow maneuver both of them out of the situation. And although he would never admit it, the thing that Bobby was actually most scared of was the prospect of meeting hungry jaguars on their way. Bobby closed his eyes and turned to his brother.

"Okay, you win. But bring all your travel gear including your pocketknife. We don't know what's going to be out there when we go."

Eli happily jumped from his bed and grabbed his Travpack.

"And for the last time, can you please go to the bathroom before we leave!"

"Oh! We'll be back in no time—don't worry," Eli said, walking away confidently.

Had Eli known what was in store for them, he would not have mentioned anything about time.

Chapter Four

"Are you sure that this is the right way?" asked Bobby uneasily, when he saw Eli stepping away from the trail path into the trees.

Going on a midnight trip in a foreign country was not something he envisioned as a "cool adventure." It was always Eli who did this kind of stuff and, after striking spider webs for about the last hour, Bobby promised himself that this would be the last time he would do such a thing.

"Yeah, I'm sure. It's actually a shortcut so we can reach Chich'en Itzá in half the time," said Eli assuredly. "Look, I know what I'm doing, okay? Just listen to me and we'll find that watch."

After another half-hour of hard trekking through the rainforest, the two finally reached the perimeter of the compound. Suddenly Eli motioned with his hand to stop moving. The brothers crept behind the trunk of a large tree.

"What?" Bobby whispered. Eli did not respond but pointed to a spot about 100 feet away. Bobby looked and gasped.

The jaguar is a stalk-and-ambush rather than a chase predator. It prefers a killing method unique amongst cats: it pierces directly through the temporal bones of the skull between the ears of a prey with its canine teeth, piercing the brain.

A large jaguar was prowling in the middle of the compound. It seemed to have heard their movements and was looking in their direction. Silently, Eli picked up a rock lying beside them.

The jaguar started moving towards them. Bobby began shaking all over. Of all the carnivores, he was most afraid of jaguars. His friends at school had found this odd because of the relative obscurity of the jaguar compared to that of the lion or tiger. But he knew the truth. Jaguars weighed up to 350 pounds, roughly the same size as the average big cat. But what separates them is their enormous bite which is strong enough to pierce even an armored animal. No other feline could match a jaguar when it came to biting.

As the jaguar got closer, Bobby saw all this in terrible detail.

No wonder the Mayans worshipped and feared the Great Jaguar god, Balam! It's easily the most powerful animal on the continent.

Suddenly the jaguar began sprinting in their direction. Bobby started to get up in order to run away but Eli held him down.

"Wait! I have an idea. It's the only way we'll make it." Crouching, he threw the stone he was holding as hard as he could into the pond on the far side of the compound. The stone made a loud splashing noise. The jaguar stood still for a moment before running off in that direction.

Eli looked at his amazed brother.

"Jaguars can't see well. They base their eyesight on motion."

"Wow... I definitely owe you one big time," said Bobby.

Eli grinned, "Come on, we don't have much time!"

They walked onto the grounds. No one was there and although Bobby was sure that countless security cameras were hidden on the premises, the two crept onto the compound.

Bobby silently followed his brother up a tattered trail until they could clearly view the huge structures of Chich'en Itzá. Even though he had seen them just hours before, their awesomeness still left him standing still, especially the great pyramid, El Castillo, as the Spanish had called it. The once paramount temple for the Mayans' religion, its smooth surface gleamed in the moonlight. What a cool way to combine architecture and astronomy. A Mayan trademark!

"Hey Bobby, are you just going to stand there or are you going to start searching for your watch?" Eli commanded.

"Okay, I'm looking." But the image of moonlight glimmering off the pyramid was still in his head.

The two split up with Eli going off to search the Great Ball Court, where the Mayans played Ulama. Ms. Fletcher had told them that Ulama is one of the oldest continuously played sports, and also is the oldest sport to utilize a rubber ball. In fact, the game is still played in some Mexican states such as Sinaloa.

TEMPLE OF THE WARRIORS. Templo de los Guerreros

Meanwhile, Bobby set off to search the Temple of Warriors. On his way, he thought back to what Ms. Fletcher said about the monument:

"The Temple of the Warriors is one of the most impressive structures in Chich'en Itzá. Built during the Late Classical Period, the temple consists of four platforms, flanked on the west and south sides by 200 round and square columns. Serpent columns engraved with astronomical and decorative figures make this one of the spectacular structures on the site."

It's amazing to think that while many parts of the world were stuck in the Dark Ages, the Mayans were so advanced, thought Bobby. *And yet, this great civilization was shattered by conquests eventually.*

A glint of silver brought his attention to the mission at hand, but it turned out to be just a candy wrapper.

The two continued to search for the watch for well over an hour until Bobby cried out,

"Hey Eli, I found it! It was under a pile of leaves but nothing's wrong with it, I think."

But Eli did not respond even when Bobby called out his brother's name several more times. Anxious, he ran across to the north side of the field where at last he saw his brother. Eli had a captivated look on his face and was staring at the top of the pyramid with his mouth wide open, in a perfect oval shape.

"Eli, for the last time can you answer when I call your name? I thought that jaguar got you!"

His brother paid no attention. Instead he whispered, in wonder, "Bobby, look at that."

"Did you even hear what I just said? Why are you standing like that—like a statue?"

"Can't you see it?" asked Eli. "At the top?"

Bobby raised his head to see the subject of his brother's fascination, but had his own breath taken away just as quickly.

At the top of the pyramid, there was a small door. But what caught the brothers' eyes was the moonlight that was passing perfectly through the door. The beam of light went through the door and curved around on the steps downward, in a serpent shape, making a shining path connecting to the serpent's head on the floor. It resembled a huge anaconda, but a magnificent one! Bobby felt as though he was in a movie studio, and not at the foot of a centuries old Mayan structure. There was something otherworldly about the sight.

Suddenly, he felt a watery tingle on his arm, a feeling unlike any that he had felt before.

"Eli, do you feel something?" he asked tensely.

"Yeah, I feel something weird!" Eli paused. "It's going all over my body now!"

Then he suddenly turned stiff as if he were indeed playing statue. Moments later, he began crying out, "Bobby, help! I CAN'T MOVE!"

The elder brother tried to remain unperturbed. Yelling would not help the situation.

"I'm feeling the same. Just stay calm. I read about something like this; I think it's called polycrystalline—nucleic formation where the lipids in your body stop functioning, causing paralysis of the entire body...All we need are two tons of frozen salt and some iodine to encase ourselves in, I think," he said, rattling away his scientific knowledge. He was pretty sure that was what Chapter 32, Lesson three of his Chemistry textbook had said.

"Well we don't have that, do we?" shouted Eli, "We need to get ou—"

But what Eli was about to say was not known because suddenly, in a bright blue flash, both boys disappeared. Only a Rolex watch on the ground remained as a sign of their existence.

Chapter Five

Mayan Soldier

Bobby opened one of his eyes to see a strange man in even stranger clothes looking at him. How bizarre!

"Eli, Eli...you there?" he whispered. He felt as though he had been squeezed and stretched out a million times, as if he had passed through a long, narrow tunnel. A tunnel with no end in sight.

Hearing no reply, Bobby got up and glanced around, but the weird looking man followed his every move. The man wore a traditional Central-American tunic of some kind with a dramatic head-dress, which made him look like somebody from a Mayan museum. His face was covered in white paint. He had a bronze sword attached to his belt and had a body of a runner, tall and lean, with laser sharp eyes. The overall effect was slightly menacing.

"Uh, do I know you?" Bobby asked warily. A mysterious man following you did not bode well most of the time.

"Who are you and who sent you? The Toltecs? Speak now and tell the truth!" demanded the man sharply, bypassing Bobby's question.

"Well, I don't know who you are so I won't answer you. Anyway, it's basic Boy Scout conduct for unfamiliar people."

He looked around hoping to see Eli. Tall trees now surrounded the area where he had been just minutes before. Something else different!

But where was his brother?

Bobby faced the stalker who seemed, upon closer inspection, to be garbed in some sort of animal hide.

"Did you see my brother? Short, chubby kid, round-faced, with a Red Sox cap?"

"Who are you and who sent you? Speak now!" shouted the man, intensely examining the boy.

Obviously, he seemed to care only about his own questions. Bobby looked away in exasperation, suddenly tired.

Finding Eli was the top priority for now. The sun was high in the sky; it must be at least noon. Their parents were probably looking for them. But he had no idea where he was.

What had happened at Chich'en Itzá?

He decided that he had to find the nearest Western Union and call his parents. To do that, he would have to ask for some basic information. Then, hopefully, everything would be fine.

But this man was clearly determined to hold him up.

Bobby turned to the man who still seemed to be stalking his every move.

"Okay, look. My name is Bobby Irukurehc from Boston, Massachusetts. Somehow my brother and I got lost. Can you tell me where the nearest Western Union is or at least show me where my brother is if you've seen him? Where are we anyway?"

The man studied Bobby even more suspiciously for some time and then said, "We do not have any unions with people from the west. Which western city were you planning on uniting with? Did they send you here?" He spoke in a probing, sharp tone.

While Bobby tried to decipher the questions, the man continued, "I personally do not know what the Western Union is so I will take you to our main city. You do not seem like a Toltec, but I have to make sure anyway. Life is harsh enough without those barbarians chasing us around."

Then in a slightly friendlier gesture, the man stretched out his hand.

"By the way, my name is Itzkas. Where are you from again?"

"Boston...Boston, Massachusetts." When the man did not say anything in acknowledgement, Bobby went on. "You know, Red Sox, Celtics, all the great sports teams."

Itzkas gave him a blank stare and shrugged his shoulders.

"Where on earth do you live to not have heard of those teams?" Bobby asked incredulously. To him, even foreigners would know about the great Boston teams.

"I live in the Yucatan Veracruz peninsula, in the great city of Chich'en Itzá," declared Itzkas.

"Veracruz?—Never heard of the place...wait...did you say that you live in Chich'en Itzá?" he asked, startled.

"Yes, that is where we Mayans live. It is a great city, for the divine Kukulcan has blessed us."

Now it was Bobby who was completely floored.

CHAPTER SIX

"Veracruz...How did I end up here?"

Then the lights flashed on in his brain. He stood still for a moment and just looked at Itzkas. It was only then that the boy became aware that his own Boston sweatshirt and jeans had been covered with traditional Mayan clothing. He ran his fingers over his chest, and felt the soft touch of Capixay, the traditional Mayan shirt, and the new animal-hide pants.

Oh my god, he thought. *No wonder Itzkas looked and acted so strangely. Somehow he and Eli were transported far back in time to the Mayan civilization of Chich'en Itzá!*

No, this can't be happening, said his rational side. *Stuff like this only happens in the movies, not to two perfectly, ordinary kids—well, if you can consider Eli to be ordinary. One moment they were looking at the moonlight and the next they were transported centuries back in time?*

A million questions began popping up in his mind. *Did it have anything to do with the Mayan prophecy of 2012? How did his clothing change and how could he even talk with Itzkas who spoke the Mayan language? Did Time Travel solve all these problems, enabling them to converse? Few things made sense.*

"Itzkas, did I appear out of nowhere when you found me?" He needed as much information as possible.

"Yes," replied Itzkas in a friendlier tone. Bobby's not being a Toltec seemed to have calmed him down. "I was about 50 feet away, when I saw two boys fall out of the sky. The plump, smaller boy immediately got up and ran away when he saw us coming, but I sent my scout after him. They are probably both at Chich'en Itzá at this moment."

So that's what happened to Eli.

"When we reach the main city, you and your brother will have to present yourselves to the Royal Council. There you must tell the truth, for falsehood pays a high price at Chich'en Itzá," warned Itzkas.

Bobby closed his eyes and resolved to stay calm. He still had no clue how he and Eli had been transported back in time. But now, regardless of what had happened, finding Eli would be his top mission. This Itzkas person seemed knowledgeable, if not affable, and being nice to him would probably be a most important next step. He would try to find out as much as possible from him, so that once he rejoined his brother, they could somehow get back.

"So, by high price you mean..." His voice quavered.

He knew the Mayans were not as violent as their northern neighbors, the Aztecs, but Itzkas's "high price" sounded ominous.

"By high price, I mean having your head chopped off," replied Itzkas solemnly.

"But what if they don't believe me? What if they think I'm lying even though I'm telling the truth?"

Itzkas looked at him in incredulous wonder. The same look Bobby's parents had given him when he told them that he wanted to be a ventriloquist when he grew up.

"They will know if you are telling the truth or lying for the Royal Council *always knows*." He looked straight into the boy's eyes, with a deep pondering look.

"They *always know*," he stressed again rather strikingly.

He could have been an actor.

Bobby looked away from Itzkas. Once again, the Mayan was freaking him out.

As the oldest boy in the family, it was always up to him to make sure that he and Eli got home safely. This time would be no different. Somehow he would have to get Eli and himself back home.

It'll be a simple search-and-rescue mission, he thought optimistically, trying to convince himself. The only difference was that the searching and rescuing operation would be over a millennium ago in an unstable Mayan civilization.

Bobby had a bad feeling about staying too long at Chich'en Itzá, but he was unsure why he felt that way. No matter what, there would be no dallying; just find Eli and go back into the future.

Itzkas motioned for him to follow down the pathway. The two walked silently, brooding over their own thoughts. The path alternated between thick forests, opening up to the outskirts of villages, and magnificent buildings in the center of town.

Are these the cities close to Chich'en Itzá*?* Bobby's mind tried to remember the names he had read in the travel brochures. *Palenque, Tikal, Mayapan, Calakmul, Tulum?* He pictured the ruins in the booklets, but what he saw now were solid, artistic structures in vibrant surroundings. *No overgrown forests hovering over these places.*

Calakmul is one of the largest ancient Maya cities ever uncovered. It is located in the 1,800,000 acre Calakmul Biosphere Reserve, deep in the jungles of the Petén, 30 km from the Guatemalan border.

They trudged for several hours until they reached a fork at the end of the road.

"We are here," said Itzkas.

Bobby, lost in his thoughts, had completely forgotten that he was trekking, but when he looked he was surprised at what he saw. From the elevated point at where they stood, he saw the same city that he had been touring the day before.

Aerial view of Chichén Itzá. The El Caracol (Venus observatory) is seen in the frame center, with the Pyramid of Kulkulkan beyond. Photo courtesy NASA, Ideum.

But it was poles apart now.

Crowds of people were weaving through the vast open plaza talking to each other or just watching the passersby. The entire scene was full of life and vibrance and the clear, blue sky added to the naturalness of the scene. Everywhere he looked, he saw Mayans walking, almost all wearing bright, colorful clothing. The women seemed to wear a decorative cotton blouse, with intricate designs near the neck. Men wore cotton breechcloths wrapped around their waist. A richly embroidered cloth hung loosely over the shoulders of many of the men and women, and moved slightly in the cool breeze. The clothing was further adorned with different types of jewelry. Bobby could see some people wearing beads, while others wore gold and fine metals.

Close-up of Mayan Ball Court Hoop. In the center, high up on each of the long walls, are ringed hoops carved with intertwining serpents.

Shops were lined up on both sides of the narrow stone streets that traversed the entire plaza. *In my time, all this is grass,* thought Bobby. Merchants were waving their goods in the air and frantically trying to sell to customers. At one end of the plaza, beside the ball court, several Mayan children were playing Ulama, hitting the round, rubber ball on their thighs and trying to send it through an imaginary hoop, just as Ms. Fletcher had described. To their right, on the real Ulama court, shouts and cheers could be heard coming from the actual game taking place. Bobby could see banners and the foreign dignitaries who were seated in tiers on the upper deck of the court. He watched as a Mayan kicked the ball through the hoop and heard the deafening applause that followed. On the other end of the plaza, several Mayan priests, dressed in clothing with signs inscribed, were conducting a ceremony of some kind over a small child, with an adoring crowd surrounding them. One priest held a small metal object and was waving it around the colorfully dressed child who could not have been more than five years old. Bobby remembered that the Mayans performed their own type of baptism before Christianity reached their shores.

There must be hundreds of people here, he thought. Itzkas motioned to him and they walked to a more elevated area behind the plaza. From here Bobby could see beyond the crowded streets of the city. Never-ending fields of maize, the staple of the Mayans' diet, extended to the horizon. They continued walking until they came back down to the center of the plaza. In the small shops, Bobby saw some familiar goods being sold, most commonly flat bread tortillas. He remembered reading about how popular tortillas were in Mesoamerica.

The gentle breeze carried with it an appetizing smell of roasting pork. Bobby saw vendors with large pans and suddenly felt a deep pang of hunger.

The gigantic Pyramid of Kukulcan and the many other lesser pyramids were still bright and shining in the sun. But upon closer inspection, something looked different.

What an erosive effect time has on ancient structures...everything looks so much more majestic! I can't believe that I am seeing it in its glory days, thought Bobby.

As he was admiring the craftsmanship, something less glamorous caught his attention. Along the side of a stone wall behind the ball court, human heads had been stored in niches. It was a wall of skulls, with stacks of heads. The wall was about two-thirds filled. Why was the other third empty? He furrowed his brow. Something about the wall gave Bobby an uneasy pang in his stomach. And pangs never were good.

Wall of skulls. Mayan's public display of human skulls, typically those of war captives or other sacrificial victims

"Welcome to Chich'en Itzá," proclaimed Itzkas.

CHAPTER SEVEN

———•———

"Bobby," someone yelled, "I can't believe you found me!"

Bobby turned around and saw his younger brother running full speed at him. For a kid with so much baby fat all around his frame, Eli could run pretty fast.

The same changes were evident in Eli. His clothing had been replaced with traditional Mayan garb; he wore a shirt of vibrant colors and multiple large bead necklaces hung around his neck. Surprisingly, Eli seemed to fit in with the rest of the Mayan people.

He actually looks better in those clothes, thought Bobby. *I can't see his round tummy in those loose robes.*

"What happened?" he asked. "Are you all right?"

"Yeah, I'm fine. I woke up before you and I saw this strange guy coming toward us. I ran away as fast I could, but he caught me and brought me here. Weird time travel, huh?"

Bobby just shook his head in astonishment. The whole ordeal still barely made any sense. They should have been eating croissants in their tent by now.

"You figured it out too? This is really messed up. We got transported back in time to Chich'en Itzá and now I have no idea about how to get back."

"Yep. Mom and Dad are probably looking for us right now... might be standing right here where we are! A thousand years into the future," remarked Eli, gesturing to the ground where they stood.

"As long as we stick together, we should be all right."

Glancing around, Bobby placed his hands on his hips and pushed the hair on his forehead back against the wind, trying to look confident to his younger brother. Itzkas was speaking with several prominent looking Mayans, who were wearing clothing of fine material embedded with shells and beads. As he spoke, he pointed to the children a couple of times. Bobby kept his eyes on Itzkas. As promised, Itzkas had united him with Eli. *Itzkas can be trusted*, he thought.

But something about Chich'en Itzá nagged at him. It was something that he had read, but he could not quite remember what it was. He could recite everything about the Roman Empire, its rise and fall. Although he knew many facts about the Mayans too, no one knew for sure how the Mayans' reign had collapsed. His mind recollected how violently many dynasties in history had ended.

Itzkas was now walking toward them and motioned for both the brothers to come closer. Bobby and Eli slowly walked over.

"We have decided that you two will be brought first before the Royal Priests for judgment. The Royal Council is busy at the moment, but they will be the final authority in determining the best path for you," said Itzkas.

"Although you do not seem to be troublesome, the priests will use the will of the gods to decide. Our honorable priests serve as intermediaries between us and the holy deities. They are very learned men; they perform all our rituals, teach the Mayan script, write our books and decipher the calendar for the rest of us. You are in good hands!"

"Okay, but after this "royal council" thing, we need some major help to get back home," said Eli. As usual, he was not afraid of asking anybody for anything, no matter the situation.

"If I don't go back into the future before "American Idol" starts, I might just cry. I worship Anoop Desai! He's like God!" continued Eli, pretending to rub tears away from his rosy cheeks.

Itzkas glanced at Eli calmly for a few seconds. Then, with great confidence, and looking at the sky, he said, "Do not despair. We have ample gods for you to worship here. If you provide the date and time of your birth, our holy priests can draw up your astrological chart, and inform you about the deity you should worship. Our priests carefully study the stars and other planetary bodies, and you will be assigned a celestial god aligned to your birth time. The time and god are very important!" Itzkas's posture was like a statue, left hand on his hip, right hand raised toward the sky, with his index finger pointing upward.

Leaving Eli standing dumbfounded, Itzkas said to Bobby, "You and your brother will follow me now."

With that, he walked toward a group of priests who were waiting in front of a stone temple at the other side of the compound. This particular temple had a rather foreboding look to it. Painted in black with red stripes across the top of the entrance, it was small and dark with torches lighting the interior. Bobby was sure that whatever was inside would not be pleasant. There was no laughter or chatter in the area, and no children or passersby were present there.

"Should we go?" asked Bobby cautiously.

"Well, it'll be better than standing out here with no help," said Eli. "Let's go, maybe the holy priests can help us--I can sing a song from 'American Idol' to impress them, and maybe dance too?"

The brothers moved toward the priests who stopped talking the moment they arrived.

"Here are the magic children," announced Itzkas.

"Magic children?" whispered Bobby incredulously.

"Well, it's better than the 'random kids from the future who fell out of the sky,'" replied Eli.

The priests conferred with each other in hushed voices and eventually the tallest, oldest priest emerged from the group.

"Young children, my name is Azumel, the high priest of Chich'en Itzá."

At least sixty years old, he had wrinkles covering his forehead. He conspicuously wore rich clothing, embellished with many different colors and jewels that separated him from the rest of the group. But something about the look in his eyes made Bobby feel wary of him.

It's probably because he is the most powerful priest, he thought.

He recollected that the Mayan priests held a very high position of authority in the kingdom. They were the king's trusted confidants. All major decisions, such as when to start a war, when to wed, and the timing of breaking ground for construction were dictated by the priests.

"Our apologies for the inconvenience, for I know that you have gone through much already. However, at this time we are having problems with our rivals, the Toltecs, and we must make sure that you bring no evil with you. Therefore, my fellow priests and I will conduct a ritual to test and cleanse you. Thankfully, it is the auspicious time, so the gods are favorable now."

Detecting concern in the boys' eyes, Azumel added, "Do not worry. Once we finish cleansing you, we will send you back to where you came from."

But Eli did not understand what Azumel had said. "Auspicious time? What does he mean by that? Our only auspicious time is when we can play the Wii or Playstation. And they don't have either, I can tell!" muttered Eli.

Meanwhile, Bobby's mind was racing toward his store of Mayan information, retrieving what he had read about the Mayans. The Mayan concept of time was different. It was the center of their lives, dictating when to do what. Every day was ruled by a god. Some days were auspicious days. On the other hand, there were days ruled by inauspicious or unlucky gods. The holy priests kept track of the complex observations, and decided the timings and the courses of action. The movement of the planets, their alignment and other information was carefully observed and recorded, and conclusions derived from them.

"So what are we going to do until we go back?" asked Eli.

Azumel looked at Eli appraisingly. "Perhaps you can tell us about your world."

Eli glanced at himself and then at Bobby.

"We seem dirty after running around through time––—we surely could use a good deep cleansing! Let's finish this "ritual" thing and get home quickly. I call soft couch for tonight's show."

Chapter Eight

Mayan Temple

Bobby and Eli walked with the priests for several minutes until they reached the entrance of the temple. On closer inspection, this building looked even more foreboding. Bobby thought he heard screaming from the inside.

"Is this it?" asked Eli. His face looked a little scared. One thing was sure: whatever was inside the temple was best left alone.

"Yes, this is the Ahaw Kin temple, one of our main Sun Gods. He will deliver your final verdict as he does for all of us" said Azumel.

"If you prove to be untrustworthy, Ahaw Kin will accept you as human offering. Then your skulls will be placed in the wall behind the Ulama courts."

Bobby looked at his brother.

"So, just don't lie! Other than that, no pressure."

Azumel adjusted his loose robes, circling them over his elbow, and bent slightly so his tall body could pass through the archway. The boys followed him, entering a long corridor.

Suddenly they stopped.

A figure was being carried out on a stretcher from the temple by two priests. But something was wrong with him. Bobby squinted his eyes and then gasped.

The man had no head! His chest was cut open, with what seemed to be a red bloody heart being carried in a small container.

"Another one gone rotten, Lihkin?" laughed Azumel. The priest bowed his head.

"At least we will not have to worry about sacrifices for Kukulcan this season."

Bobby gulped apprehensively.

They continued walking inside until they approached the edge of the pit. Bobby recognized it from one of his books. They were at the edge of the Cenote.

The Yucatan Peninsula has almost no rivers and only a few lakes. The Cenote was a 1,000-foot hole in the ground that was at times the Mayans' only access to quality freshwater. The Cenote was also used as a testing ground for future kings and as a chamber where sacrifices took place.

"Bring them together and place them over the pit of Ahaw Kin," ordered Azumel sternly.

Two priests tied Eli and Bobby to long bamboo poles and lowered them into the pit, just next to the Cenote.

"Bobby, will we be okay?" asked Eli queasily. Listening to the priests suddenly did not seem so enticing.

"Yes, don't worry!"

Bobby did not want to scare his brother in these circumstances, knowing that both of them could end up like the man just carried out. The picture of the red bloody heart filled his mind. He could not imagine his little brother being tied up and ... *Oh! No! I can't think this way. Just like in the movies, you had to be cool and level-headed to survive.* He looked down at the pit and saw fires at the bottom rising. Never mind.

"Bobby!" yelled Eli.

The priests were now chanting loudly and raising their hands. Bobby could not help but feel that he was in some Sci-Fi movie. But he knew that the experience was all too real. And something which many people did not survive. He shuddered at that thought. *I need to be strong. A scout is strong! Yes – A Scout is strong. I am a Boy Scout and I am strong.*

"Eli! Listen to me. Don't ever look down. Just keep looking at me" Bobby commanded. With a scared face and beads of sweat dripping from his forehead, Eli nodded.

"Ahaw Kin will now decide your fate," shouted Azumel above the din. The fire became even fiercer, and intense blue lights flashed around them. Nothing seemed to be following the laws of science.

The fire erupted and a bright orange flash lit up the entire pit. Then silence.

"Eli, you okay?" asked Bobby anxiously.

"Yeah, I'm fine. But what on earth was that?" remarked Eli.

Bobby felt as if a dizzying roller-coaster ride had ended. He strained his head to the side to the extent that the ropes would allow. New messengers had come in and were converging around Azumel, whispering. The high priest nodded and pointed toward Bobby and Eli. After a few moments, he hurried toward the brothers.

"Our king calls for us. You must come with us to the palace quickly. Bad news has arrived and you may be of use."

"But are we safe?" asked Bobby.

"Yes. You have passed the test of treachery. You are who you say you are. Now you are one of us."

Eli's eyes opened wide, filled with surprise. After a couple of priests pulled up the poles and untied the ropes around the brothers' arms, Eli ran toward his brother, panting.

"One of them?" he whispered, "We are not one of them. Bobby! Do you hear me? We are not one of them! We need to get home. Mom and Dad are probably over their heads searching for us."

Bobby noticed a shadow of uneasiness in his eyes.

"You're right. But Azumel said something bad has happened. He also said he needed our help. Unless we can fix it, I have a feeling it's going to be some time before we reach home," said Bobby.

The brothers strode along with Azumel and the rest of the priests for several minutes until they reached the citadel of Chich'en Itzá. The evening sun glancing over the sides of the buildings made the city look even grander.

As they walked they were joined by Itzkas who informed the brothers what had just happened.

"One of our patrols was ambushed while it was scouting around the northern city of Edzna. His Highness, the Royal Emperor Topiltzin believes that the Toltecs were behind the attack. There were no survivors.

"Although we have had the occasional fight, our conflict with the Toltecs has mostly remained diplomatic. Brazen attacks are not a good sign."

Itzkas closed his eyes and looked up at the sky. "In fact it has been the fifth ambush this year."

Azumel joined the conversation. "If I didn't know better, I would think that someone from our side is giving information to the Toltecs. How else could they carry out so many attacks?" He spat in disgust.

Itzkas turned to one of his scouts whom Bobby noticed had only one ear. All that was left of the other was a gaping hole. *I wonder how that happened,* he thought.

"Did they leave anything, Harappan?" asked Itzkas.

"They left a note saying that more ambushes would come if they did not receive land and money from His Highness," replied Harappan.

This statement was met with a sound of disbelief from Itzkas.

"What can we do? We have already had a drought and a bad harvest. King Topiltzin is right; we cannot give any more to these barbarians. Our people will suffer even more if we do."

"Who are the Toltecs?" asked Eli. Ms. Fletcher had briefly mentioned them but not in any great detail.

"The Toltecs are a savage people from the north who are mainly skilled warriors. We Mayans are a learned, civilized people. We spend time studying and recording the movements of the celestial bodies in the universe, especially of Tzolkin.[2] Even our great temples are positioned and designed so they can be used as observatories. We have gathered a large amount of information, which allows us to envision the future of the earth and major events. Our priests can foretell what Mother Nature has in store for us and predict the good and bad times. Almost everything we know is based on the relative positions of the planets." Itzkas' deep voice reflected a sense of pride.

---

2   The Mayan Word for Venus

El Caracol - Mayan Venus Observatory. The grand staircase that marks the front of El Caracol faces 27.5 degrees north of west which is out of line with the other buildings at the site, but an almost perfect match for the northernmost position of Venus. Photo courtesy NASA, Ideum

"But warfare is not one of our strong points. Years ago we formed an alliance with the Toltecs to fight against our common enemies. But now they want more, while we can afford to give less and less. We have already had small conflicts in the past, but I fear for a full-scale war," replied Itzkas.

Bobby whispered to his brother, "I remember hearing about the Toltecs now...they did something bad, but I can't remember what."

Eli looked troubled and said quietly, "Yeah, me too, and according to Itzkas, they attacked the Mayan patrols."

He turned back to Itzkas. "Can't you make a pact with them?"

"No. We cannot give anything more. Chich'en Itzá is already overpopulated and we have been plagued with diseases. Let us hope that cooler minds prevail and the Toltecs do not attack anymore!"

Bobby couldn't agree more. Chich'en Itzá had indeed looked overpopulated with hundreds of people crowded into one citadel. "But do not distress yourselves with our worries. You must go to the palace now. King Topiltzin will want to know much about you," said Itzkas in a more cheerful voice.

"Your knowledge may be able to help us." Azumel's voice boomed from behind.

"Let's go, Eli. As long as we stick together, we should be fine," said Bobby, squeezing his brother's hand in reassurance.

Itzkas stood by and watched as Azumel led the brothers toward the palace, shining red under the setting sun.

CHAPTER NINE

Wall/Door Carvings

The guards positioned on either side of the intricately carved doors of the palace slowly pulled them open as the group arrived. Known as the Palace of Ahau Balam Kauil, it had two levels and large stone friezes depicting jaguars. The entire palace was circular shaped and surrounded a flourishing courtyard which gave it an aesthetic and natural look. Just like the Pyramid of Kukulcan, the Palace of Ahau Balam Kauil had looked more worn in the future.

Once inside the palace, Azumel, Bobby and Eli walked to a central court where the King and royalty were sitting. Elaborate paintings and sculptures filled the interior of the walls.

Mayan Mask

"We have arrived, Your Majesty," declared Azumel.

King Topiltzin in traditional attire

King Topiltzin turned from his audience. Even from a distance, Bobby could make out that he must be the king. He was a very tall and muscular man and held a commanding presence that would cow even the most confident of men. The clothes he wore were quite opulent and were adorned in ornaments of gold and precious stones. He head was covered with a huge traditional head-dress. The other royalty wore rich clothes, but with fewer precious jewels.

King Topiltzin gestured toward them to take their places.

"I trust that you have heard the news," said the king, immediately addressing Azumel. The report of the recent attack had reached the highest ranks.

"Yes, Your Majesty," replied Azumel. The high priest took his seat beside the King while the brothers stood in the center of the court. "The Toltecs must be dealt with swiftly before they become too powerful."

"That is a matter that we have to decide," said the King. He had a thoughtful expression on his handsome face.

Bobby sensed that the King was not a man to make rash decisions about war. His thoughts returned to the troubled world back home.

How peaceful would my world be if every nation had leaders who were cautious about war.

Now King Topiltzin cast his gaze upon Bobby and Eli.

"Who are these young visitors? I do not recall ever seeing them in Chich'en Itzá. Their clothes are our attire, but their faces look different."

"They are newcomers to this land. Ahaw Kin has already determined that they are clean, so they cannot be Toltecs. Apparently they are from the future, yet somehow they ended up here," replied Azumel.

The princes whispered in disbelief and some in awe. But the King did not seem as surprised by Azumel's statement.

"Well, if you are from the future, what year do you live upon Earth?" asked King Topiltzin.

"Two Thousand Ten, Your Majesty," said Bobby.

The king raised his brow, then looked Bobby in the eye for a few seconds. He glanced at the rest of his Court with a knowing expression. Bobby noticed that the members of court shifted uncomfortably in their seats and began whispering to each other upon hearing the year. They observed Bobby and Eli with a certain pity on their faces.

Azumel looked quizzically at the brothers.

"Child, in your world, do you know that our Mayan calendar ends at 2012?" he asked. "Perhaps, you may have been experiencing abnormal natural catastrophes?"

Bobby thought back to the past year. True, disasters like the tsunamis, great oil spill and the Asian floods had wreaked havoc, but few actually believed that the events had anything to do with 2012.

"Yes, we heard, but no one believes it," piped up Eli, echoing Bobby's belief. Turning to the king, Eli continued, "Anyway, what can we do to get out of here? That's *our* main problem, you know."

Eli is not afraid of anyone. He continues to speak his mind, as if he were in his own living room, thought Bobby.

But the king did not seem offended by Eli's audaciousness and lack of trust in the sacred Mayan calendar. "Don't worry. Our priests will sort out your problem," he replied, looking a bit amused by Eli.

Before the king could continue the conversation, new council members arrived and were sitting with the other princes at the round table. Many looked gaunt and talked in hushed voices.

"Those Toltec people seem to be very bad," remarked Eli, grasping the mood of the Royal Council.

"King Topiltzin, what are we going to do?" asked one of the princes.

"We will decide that matter at a later time," replied the King. "Right now, we have two special guests here, children from the future."

Bobby and Eli greeted the newcomers and, at the king's invitation, explained their predicament. Although initially the reactions were mixed with disbelief, once they heard that Ahaw Kin had checked them, the council members unanimously believed the brothers' story.

"So you need help to get back home? Our priests should fix that. Is that correct, Azumel?" asked one prince. Azumel bowed his head in agreement, his brow deeply furrowed in thought.

King Topiltzin waved for Bobby and Eli to leave so that he could discuss serious matters with the members of court.

"I will call you back soon," said the King.

Azumel motioned the children to follow him and they walked toward the large doors. The guards pulled the doors open as they approached and a sudden gust of wind entered the room, like an uninvited guest waiting to enter a party. Bobby's hair was swept back, and the loose front of his Mayan robes blown apart by the wind, revealing his modern clothing underneath.

As he tried to pull the robe together, one of the princes seated near the doors cried out, "Stop!"

Bobby and Eli turned to look at the prince, a squat little man with pudgy hands and a belly the size of a walrus.

"What's that on your clothing?" the prince demanded loudly, pointing toward Bobby's shirt.

For a few moments Bobby did not have a clue about what the prince referred to, and looked over to an equally confused looking Eli.

One of the chiefs yelled out, "Answer Prince Itzamma, you xiipals![3]" before King Topiltzin calmed him and pointed at Bobby.

------

3   Boys, underlings

"Prince Itzamma is referring to those letters on your clothing. What do they mean?"

Comprehension dawned upon Bobby as he realized they were talking about the words on his shirt, which read "Cuidado con el futuro".

"Oh, it's nothing really. I bought this shirt when my family visited Barcelona, you know, in Spain."

A sudden buzz like angry bees spread through the room as the princes talked to each other, with frowns upon their faces. Some were fingering their swords. The king gazed at the boys steadily and then also grimaced. Folding his hands behind him, he rose and began to pace back and forth, his face locked in serious thought.

After a minute he asked, "Did you hear about the ambush on one of our patrols before you two showed up?"

The boys nodded, for Itzkas had told them about it.

"Well, it so happened that we found a man who took a hit from our arrows, lying on the ground. He had some of the same words in a book in his bag."

The King paused to see if his statement had any effect on the brothers.

"We heard that such men had arrived in the north a long time ago for trading. The local people provided help during their temporary stays. But they have never ventured down here, until this ambush."

Bobby stared in horror at his own shirt and then at the men assembled in the room. So that was why they had had to go through the purification process, so that the priests could check whether they were spies for any new enemy.

But why would the words on a shirt that Bobby bought in a modern bookstore in Barcelona appear centuries earlier in a place thousands of miles away? Bobby gazed at his brother who seemed to be thinking the same thing.

Then slowly, he began to understand.

Turning to his brother, Bobby whispered so the Mayans could not hear. "Eli, remember Ms. Fletcher had said something about the Spanish? I forget whether it was good or bad--"

"Francisco de Cortoba!" replied Eli.

"Who?"

"Francisco de Cortoba. A Spaniard who led expeditions into the Mayan heartland in search of gold. I forgot whether it was 1497 or 1517, but I remember that some major fights happened until the Spanish took full control of the Yucatan Peninsula."

Eli looked at his amazed brother.

"Don't ask me how I know all this extra stuff. Mom made me read about it after I snuck out to Edmund's house to play on his new Playstation. It's coming back to me now. The book was somewhat nice if you skipped the parts about human sacrifice and hearts stuck on spears."

Ignoring the excess information, Bobby gasped.

"The Spanish attacked the Mayans!"

So that's why the patrol had seen the words when they discovered the attacker. The Spanish had arrived in the New World.

He struggled to grasp this momentous information.

Christopher Columbus discovered the New World in 1492. So, they must have arrived here sometime in the sixteenth century. Four centuries before their own time.

Eli closed his eyes and groaned, "Oh no, we arrived in the middle of a bloody war!"

Bobby looked at King Topiltzin who was now talking quietly to one of his advisers. He remembered everything now, everything that he read and heard was coming back to him in reels of flashback; how the Mayans, after they were already weakened by the Toltecs, were attacked by the Spanish as part of their conquest of the Americas; how the Spanish first came to do business with the Mayans but later began to fight for control over the land and people; how the Mayans had endured the onslaught at first but finally succumbed to the Spanish, who were more advanced in warfare; how the Mayans were exposed by the Spanish to new diseases such as smallpox, to which the natives had no resistance. Thousands of native people were wiped out as a consequence of the wars and from new diseases. Later, more were killed under the rule of tyrants such as Pedro de Alvarado and Francisco de Montejo.

Oh No! The Spaniards have arrived! This is a major war! And the Mayans have no clue about what will happen, thought Bobby. Indeed, the King and the rest of the Court seemed to have no idea of their impending misfortune. *First, they were to be tricked with friendly trading and then conquered by war. What the history books would call "victims of European colonization,"* thought Bobby sadly.

But should I tell them now and alert them?

No, said the pragmatic side of his brain, *Why would a few ambushes lead to a war? They could settle their disputes diplomatically. They'll think you're some kind of deranged lunatic and will kill you for sure.*

Then the moral side responded, *But if you don't tell them, thousands of people will die. You could help change their fate.*

Besides, King Topiltzin won't consider you important, and you will be left with the masses and be slaughtered when the Spanish attack.

Bobby decided what he had to do. He turned to his brother. "We have to tell them--or King Topiltzin at least, about what's going to happen."

Everyone else in the room was now leaning forward in their chairs, watching the brothers intently.

Eli looked uncertain for a moment, but then replied, "Yes, we should. They *need* to know."

Bobby saw a certain resolve and firmness in Eli's eyes. He patted his brother and then walked toward the king.

"King Topiltzin...could we talk to you for a moment? We think we know why you're being attacked."

"You say that you know who is attacking my people?"

Before Bobby could respond, Azumel cried out, "The king is extremely busy, and you must not waste his time. Let us leave now, so His Highness can tend to more serious matters."

Everyone in the room turned to the old priest.

Bobby did not let go of the King's attention. He had to plan carefully what he said next.

"I know I am only a kid, but I am from the future, and I read about the Mayans. That's how I know who's attacking you. These people are not your usual enemies, like the Toltecs. Your attackers are from another continent entirely and they did not come here to trade stories. They will--"

But before he could continue, King Topiltzin motioned sharply with his hand for Bobby to stop speaking.

"Stop! Do not speak any further!" he said firmly.

Bobby was silent but looked questioningly at the king.

Why doesn't he want to hear any more information?

"If you say any more, and we hear it, you will risk the future being changed. The Mayans are a religious race and whatever Kukulcan decides will happen. Good or bad, we must follow Kukulcan's fate for us. We cannot hear it from any other source, as he is our supreme power!"

The King allowed Bobby and Eli some time to absorb what he had said.

"Thankfully, it seems that your appearance has not caused too much of a disruption."

The brothers looked at each other in wonder.

What type of king does not want to hear information that could help him? Here I am--I could tell him how it is all going to unfold, then the Mayans could plan for the worst, thought Bobby.

He ran his fingers through his tousled hair in bewilderment. Then it dawned on him why what the king said was so unusual.

Of course! I come from the age of greed and corruption. A single day does not pass without hearing about political scandals, and about our elected officials' licentiousness. Ethical leadership is almost nonexistent, fading faster than the night stars under the brightness of the sun.

Bobby thought back to the story of Edwin Thatchery Hood III. A descendant of the great Robin Hood, Edwin decided to reverse what his famous namesake had represented. Literally. Instead of giving money to the poor, Edwin, an elected official, tricked and stole money from the lower classes. Then he promptly gave this money to his friends in the London banking business to invest, and kept some to build himself a miniature golf course. A true display of moral indecency.

Probably the reason why my school has to have a course on Ethics.

At that moment, Bobby felt his respect for the King and the Mayans multiply exponentially. *What a virtuous king! Even his high priest is so honorable; Azumel tried to stop me before I could utter a single word.*

God! Please help these people! The Mayans have entrusted their fate to you--please, please protect them now!

"It seems that the best course of action would be for my priests to transport you back to the future as quickly as possible. Spending any more time here would be detrimental for both parties." King Topiltzin's voice resounded, breaking into Bobby's thoughts.

The king turned to his high priest.

"Azumel, how much longer do your priests need to send these children back?"

The high priest had calmed down but was looking at Bobby uneasily.

You can relax--I am not going to say anything about the future. I respect your traditions and will keep my mouth shut, thought Bobby.

"I am afraid I do not know, my lord. The correct astrological signs must be there and my priests need more time to correct the potion. The last thing we want is to transport the children to the wrong period," replied the priest.

"Very well. Until then, provide them lodging in the palace. Let the scout who found them be in charge of showing them around Chich'en Itzá. But do not let them interfere in any important business, for that could have dire consequences."

Azamul bowed and gestured toward Bobby and Eli.

"Now farewell, my friends! I have important business."

Outside the palace, the sky had grown darker; night was rapidly approaching. The city was flickering with light here and there emanating from firewood.

Itzkas greeted the three of them happily at the bottom of the steps. The scout seemed to have bitten his lips in anxiousness. "Good! You are fine! Not many people survive the Royal Council," joked Itzkas.

"Yeah, we just made it out," replied Eli.

Azumel cleared his throat. "Itzkas, I trust you know what to do?"

The scout nodded.

"Good. Make sure you take excellent care of them. I want them to be safe and protected at all times."

The high priest walked slowly back to the temple.

Itzkas motioned for the brothers to come with him.

"Follow me. I will take you to your lodgings. Tomorrow, I will show you the best parts of this great city. By the time the priests are ready, you will not want to leave."

No one knew how true Itzkas's statement would turn out to be.

The three walked for several minutes until they reached a separate part of the Palace. Itzkas decided to elaborate on its history.

"The palace was fully completed a couple of centuries back, when Topiltzin's ancestor Topiltzac was king. His rule was a time of peace and growth and our borderlands were the furthest then. It is one of the largest and most ornate buildings in the city and houses most of the nobles and elite. Although the building is just two stories, it consists of many chambers and several interior courtyards. All in all, it is probably the most luxurious residence in all of the Yucatan."

"Where do all of the other Mayans live?" asked Bobby.

"There are many lands to the south and west which you have not seen. A great many of our people live there. They farm various vegetables and fruits. Some own farmlands, while others do not, but everyone grows their own gardens in their backyards. We Mayans like to eat fresh vegetables every day. Here in Chich'en Itzá, the common Mayans live in small huts near where they work. We have defined roles for everyone. The women cook, clean, weave, and work mostly at home and sometimes in the fields. The men perform the more arduous outdoor tasks. It is very important that these Mayans remain healthy and safe because not only do they grow the crops, but they also provide the manual labor that is needed to obtain limestone from the local quarries. And without limestone, we cannot build any of these other great structures that you see here."

They finally arrived at their room. In truth it looked more like a suite. It was about three times the size of their normal bedroom and much more extravagantly decorated. The walls were covered with gold and silver shaped like stars. Light colored, filmy curtains along the doorways and windows were moving gently with the cool night breezes. On the floor, there were two fluffy cotton beds with brightly colored sheets, alongside an intricately carved small table. At the side was a large door, presumably to the courtyard that Itzkas had talked about. The scent of sweet flowers wafted through the room from the courtyard.

"I hope this is enough?" asked Itzkas.

Bobby and Eli smiled at each other.

"Yep," they replied in unison.

"Good. Tomorrow you will be awakened promptly at dawn. Our days start really early, around four at predawn. Then I will take you to our most prized locations." Itzkas walked to the door.

"Sleep well. You have travelled much today."

Boy! That sure is an understatement, thought Bobby.

"Thanks, Itzkas," replied Bobby and Eli.

After he left, Bobby immediately fell onto the bed.

"What a day," remarked Eli.

"Indeed."

"Itzkas is a decent guy. I think he'll take good care of us until the priests are ready."

"Hopefully."

"Now I think we should just sleep."

"Good idea."

With that, the two brothers drifted into sleep, letting the darkness absorb them.

Chapter Ten

Days turned into weeks. Weeks turned into months. Then months turned into years. The boys' lanky arms now were filled out with well developed muscles.

On this day, one hot summer afternoon several years into their stay, the brothers strolled toward the plaza to attend a party King Topiltzin was holding in their honor.

"Time definitely has flown past, hasn't it, Eli?"

"Yes, it has," replied Eli. "Our parents have probably given up searching for use by now. After all, it's been a long time."

"Yeah! I wish they could know that we're having a good life here; it's really been like a long Boy Scout summer camp. I just hope they're not feeling sorrowful about us." Bobby's voice trailed off in sadness.

"Anyway, we've grown accustomed to Mayan culture. In fact, I'd say we're even liking our life here." Eli tried to cheer up the conversation.

The last statement was true. On the second day of their stay several years ago, Itzkas had shown and described many aspects of Mayan life to the boys to make them more accustomed to their new surroundings. Bobby still remembered as if it were yesterday his feelings of awe. As he came closer to the same plaza, he thought back to what Itzkas had told him years ago.

"We Mayans are obsessed with time, and our entire culture and life revolves around it. Our priests, and a lot of our resources are focused on keeping precise astronomical observations. We study the cosmos and its gradual changes and do complex calculations. Our priests are able to create calendars way into the future, up to your time."

"Why did your priests stop the calendar at 2012?" Eli chipped in.

"That is a question I cannot answer, I am not born into the upper class of priests. I am being trained to be a warrior." He continued, "We take care to record the data onto carved monuments called stelae, so that it is saved permanently. You can find these stelae throughout the Yucatan peninsula. Also--see this tree?"

He touched gently a wild fig tree. "We use the inner bark of this tree as parchment on which to write."

Stelae were essentially stone banners raised to glorify the king, record his deeds, and mark the end of calendrical cycles.

"For the Mayans, time is not just a passing measurement; time has quality associated with it. The concept of time is so important for us that sometimes royal pregnancies are even timed with an eye toward the most auspicious dates to ensure a bright future for the king and the kingdom. Wars are not fought during certain times, as the gateways to the underworld are open then. Marriages take place only during good times."

"How can you keep track of so many numbers? You don't have a super computer--do you? Math is hard enough even in fifth grade without a calculator," Eli remarked, with a confused look on his face.

Math was Eli's least favorite subject. He would rather spend his time with his globe.

Itzkas gave Eli a blank stare, and then went on to describe the number system the Mayans used which helped them calculate huge numbers with relative ease.

"We Mayans believe that everything on earth is connected to the cosmos through the energy flowing within us. Our elders and priests tell us that there are three worlds--the heaven, the earth, and the underworld. If we point to the heaven with our fingers, we are connected to the celestial realm, and our toes well grounded on the earth connect us to the underworld. This creates the energy that runs through our body, and connects us to the other worlds. So our ten fingers and the ten toes give us the number 20. The 13 jointed areas in our body reflect 13 key points in the galaxy, and connect us to the cosmos." He took a pause, pointing his fingers to the sky, as if needing to be connected to the heavens.

"That is why the numbers 20 and 13 are important to us. See--ten fingers and ten toes--so twenty, easy to teach to our children," he said, spreading out his fingers and smiling.

"So, we use a number system of base 20, also known as a vigesimal system. The advantage of this is that numbers become large extremely quickly with place values increasing exponentially going from 20 to

400 to 8000 to 160,000. See how rapidly they increase? This helps us manipulate large numbers for our astronomical calculations and Kukulcan's predictions way into the future. That is why you children could not tell us about what you know, for then the future would change and all that Kukulcan had planned for us would also change."

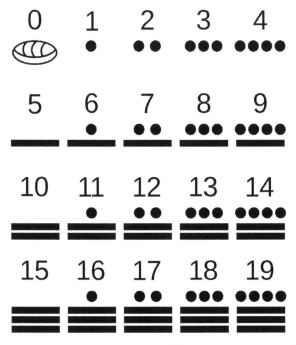

Maya numerals were a vigesimal (base-twenty) numeral system. The numerals are made up of three symbols; zero (shell shape), one (a dot) and five (a bar).

Maybe we should use base 20 instead of our base 10 to keep track of our federal deficit. It sure is getting hard to count all those trillions of dollars, thought Bobby. He was very interested in current events; back home, he would run down to the end of his driveway each morning to fetch the newspaper so he could keep up with global affairs.

"We also use the number 20 for counting days--we have 20- day cycles. The 20-day cycles are the embodiments of the gods of time or the 20 faces of the sun. Each of these 20-day signs also has 13 different variations, again the 13 key points of the galaxy. So 13 times 20 gives the 260-day cycle called the Tzolkin. It's a sacred almanac from which predictions and prophecies can be made.

"The concept is difficult to understand at first, but you will eventually know and appreciate it."

Itzkas has so many skills--he could easily be a tour guide, a teacher, as well as a skilled warrior, thought Bobby.

Next, Itzkas led them to a game of Ulama that was taking place at the edge of the plaza. He explained that Ulama ball courts could be found in almost every Mesoamerican city because the sport was extremely popular and had been played for many centuries. It was taken extremely seriously and Itzkas described how before a game, each team would sacrifice human flesh to appease the gods. The game had political importance too, as disputes were settled sometimes with a game, with the losing team sacrificed. Although the custom was gruesome, Bobby understood that such sacrifices were not unusual for the time. After all, the Romans forced humans and animals to fight to the death just for the amusement of spectators.

Before the troubles began, teams from the Toltecs and even from the Inca would come to play the Maya. Today at the game, the players ran across the ball court, bouncing the ball off their thighs and trying to get it through the stone hoop. Whenever someone scored, one side of the crowd cheered while the other groaned. The large Ulama ball was made of rubber and could weigh up to an alarming four kilograms; the players had to score using only their thighs and legs.

Thus Eli was quick to notice how muscular the Mayans' thighs were, even compared to modern-day football players.

Mayan sacrificial rite

For a while, the boys stood there watching the hundreds of people in the crowd maniacally cheering and the men playing with sweat pouring off their bodies. The royals were seated high up inside the erected walls. Luckily, it was a friendly match so that no one had to be sacrificed.

Soon their tour was finished and Itzkas went back to his duties.

But as the next several weeks passed, one thing kept dogging Bobby. The priests were making no headway in finding a way to send the brothers back to the future. The solution should have been found within a couple of weeks and, though full moons had come and passed, Azumel kept on insisting that something was still wrong. This surprised King Topiltzin a little.

"Why is it so difficult to find a way back? Did you not tell me that all you needed were the auspicious astrological signs and perhaps a potion or magical device? Surely, a correct combination of those should be at hand."

"Yes, my lord," Azumel replied. "But I'm afraid that there are many minute details which the regular Mayan would not heed, but to which a priest must pay close attention. And as I said before, the last thing we would want to do would be to send the children to the wrong time period or have them lost in the cosmos which would be even more disastrous."

So to pass the time, Itzkas sent the pair to a nearby farm to help the farmers harvest maize. "Manual labor will make you stronger. The way you look now, no one will give you any respect," joked Itzkas.

As the years passed, Itzkas himself moved up steadily in the Mayan army. He had been promoted from a scout to other intermediate positions, and had just been promoted to General of the Third Battalion for his work in securing the northern border. Now, he would remain close-by unless a full-blown war began. Over the years, the brothers and he had become very close friends.

And so the brothers grew into Mayan life. They continued working in the fields. They grew more appreciative of bucolic living and understood the hardships and pleasures of their new friends. Strong muscles formed on their bodies as Itzkas had promised. Bobby's younger brother, once a jovial, hilarious character, now acted in a much more serious manner. Inevitably, all the exposure to the Mayans and their problems had hardened him.

———————————

Several years pass

Some major things have changed, thought Bobby, as he came back to the present.

More and more people were migrating to Chich'en Itzá from different Mayan settlements. Recently, a small group of men from the coastal town of Lamanal in the south, along with their wives and children, had come to Chich'en Itzá. Their leader, a wizened old man named Chiccan, begged to immediately see King Topiltzin. Before the royal court, he spoke of a new growing menace that had come from the sea.

"My men saw them sporadically for several years trading with other small towns along the coast. They said they came from the lands beyond the far seas. Many of them sometimes looked so famished, that my people provided food and shelter for them. But just a couple of months ago, they appeared in large numbers and began building settlements along the coast, without our permission. After a couple of weeks, some of their men came to my palace requesting my presence. This was the first time I personally laid eyes on them; they ride on creatures that I had never seen before but had heard of. They did not have any weapons except for some strange sticks which they carried."

At this, King Topiltzin said, "Yes, my men have also occasionally happened on these men. They looked different, and were foraging in my kingdom. They were scared off after a couple of arrows were shot in warning. However, they were extremely few in number and did not cause any harm so we did not pay much attention to them."

Chiccan smiled weakly and said, "I thought the same as well. But everything changed when about a week ago, a group of these men walked into my palace and demanded more land and precious gold."

Several of the council members cried out in anger.

King Topiltzin, however, remained impassive.

Chiccan continued, "In my 60 years, I had never seen such insolence. Such was my anger that I sliced their leader's head off with my sword. Even some of my own men were surprised by my rage."

"You taught them a lesson about respect. So, why did you journey up here to Chich'en Itzá?" asked King Topiltzin.

Now the elderly Chiccan shook his head and several tears glistened in his eyes.

"I thought I had taught them a well-deserved lesson too. But after I killed their leader, the remainder of his men, about 20 or so, ran back to the entrance and raised their sticks up in the air. At this, my guardsmen laughed since those sticks were not sharp and could not do much harm. Then, right when my men charged, huge sounds, like lightning, and smoke appeared from the enemies' sticks. You see--these were not mere sticks that they were carrying; they had something in them...something that has never appeared in this land. My men fell like powerless children in the face of their fire. I only lived to tell the tale because my sons covered my retreat. But alas, they too fell down under that murderous fire."

Spanish attack on Lamanal

The King's council fell silent at these words.

"Guns! They are talking about rifles!" whispered Eli urgently.

Bobby and Eli looked at each other. Both of them knew that they were the only two in the room who understood the power of guns, which the Mayans had never seen before. But they had made a promise to King Topiltzin before the altar of Kukulcan to reveal nothing about the future. Though initially Bobby considered such religious obedience rather silly, he grew to understand that Kukulcan meant almost everything to the Mayans. Whether it was for a good harvest or a successful battle, the Feathered Serpent, as it was sometimes called, was all powerful. And if the god wanted the Mayans to suffer for some time, then the Mayans had to suffer.

Chiccan continued his tragic tale.

"What happened next? Horror that words alone cannot capture. The warning bell was sounded, but the foreign men were a step ahead of us. They had surrounded the city and were destroying the outside walls with huge barrels of fire. In just a couple of hours, the southern and eastern parts of the city had been burned down. The people with me are the only survivors of the tragedy at Lamanal."

At this, most of the younger council members leapt to their feet and began shouting in anger at their neighbor's fate. Several of the aged leaders sat upright in their seats with grim faces, still trying to comprehend the situation.

"But Chiccan! There were over two thousand people living in Lamanal. It is one of our largest cities after Chich'en Itzá!"

Chiccan sadly replied, "These are the last," as he pointed toward the group behind him.

Afterwards, the Royal Council conferred on the next course of action.

"There is a troubling trend. These foreigners have weapons far more powerful than anything we have seen. Furthermore, they seem to be ruthless in getting what they want. They must be stopped at all costs," said Prince Chibirias.

"I agree," replied King Topiltzin. "We are still the most powerful kingdom in Mesoamerica. Our land stretches from Coba in the north to Quiriqua in the south. However, we must not lose our vigilance to these foreigners who might take our place and rule with brutality over our people."

The King stopped for a moment before adding, "If we are to fight, then we must do so soon. For my power is not as great as my father's. The population here has grown to capacity and we have had to resort to cutting down vast swaths of forest to grow enough food. The weather has also not been favorable for agriculture. The circumstances have weakened us considerably from our past, almost impregnable, strength."

Some of the younger princes shifted in discomfort as their King continued highlighting the Mayans' weaknesses.

"The Toltecs have noticed our decline which explains their resurgent attacks on our borders over the past decade. For all we know, the Toltecs could be interacting with the foreigners. The last thing we need is for these two to ally."

Noticing the somber mood in the room, the king continued in a lighter tone, "Wars have always been there, and we have always found ways to overcome them and thrive. Let us discuss this matter at a later time. The festival of Tzolkin is upon us tomorrow, and it coincides with Bobby's and Eli's coming to this city. We will celebrate with much splendor!"

The festival of Tzolkin marked the ending of the 260-day Mayan calendar. A 584-day calendar was also maintained although it was considered less important. Tzolkin was one of the most important Mayan holidays as it marked the end of one year and the beginning of a new auspicious one.

As he walked away from the palace, Bobby gazed at two Mayan children playing Ulama, completely at ease from the happenings in the borderlands. *The King is also trying to use this celebration to calm his people, Bobby thought.*

But the story of Lamanal was spreading like wildfire and was the cause of much distress.

CHAPTER ELEVEN

Forest Slash and Burn practice

When Bobby and Eli arrived at the festival the next day, huge banners were being unfurled and the loud drums began beating.

"Bobby and Eli! How the years have passed!" called out King Topiltzin. All traces of concern that had appeared during the encounter with Chiccan the previous day were gone. The king seemed determined to conceal all of his worry.

"Did you know," asked King Topiltzin, addressing several of his ministers, "that these young men have helped increase maize production by 25%? They showed our farmers a couple of tricks on irrigation and planting seeds. I still remember when they were two lost, helpless children."

"Thank you," replied the brothers.

It was true that they had helped with the farming techniques of Chich'en Itzá. With a rapidly increasing population, it was imperative to grow as much food as possible. Bobby was surprised to learn that the Mayans did not practice crop rotation, and instead farmed the land for maize year round. They were forced to slash and burn forests to produce more quality soil, for their existing farmland lost nutrients easily. With crop rotation, more minerals in the earth could be preserved, the rate at which forests were cut down was reduced, and different food could be grown year round. Yet even with these techniques, as population from other regions crowded into Chich'en Itzá, the capital, the need to grow more and more food was rapidly erasing the forests.

Bobby and Eli spent the rest of the day playing a friendly match of Ulama which was only slightly dampened by Eli's getting hit in the head and knocked out for a few minutes. Tired and sweaty, they quickly bathed at the palace and dressed in formal Capixays, the traditional Mayan shirt, before heading back outside. They had learned by now that for participating in any Mayan ceremony, they needed to be pure. Even all the objects used, such as prayer utensils, were cleaned for each occasion. New clothes were worn if possible, and even the poor received garments for these occasions.

A feast had been prepared in the center of the plaza, with plates of food laid out on a long wooden table. The air was filled with the unique aroma of the incense made from a tree resin called *copal*. The gods were first offered fruits and delicacies, before everyone else.

"There is not as much food as usual," remarked Eli, looking at the table.

"The weather has not been favorable this season. The Toltecs have been more brazen than usual, too. I heard that in border cities such as Palenque, people are starving because of the blockade by the Toltecs," replied Bobby.

"I hope this does not have anything to do with the Spanish presence. Both you and I heard what Chiccan said."

Bobby nodded, and the notion of war brought his mind back to old thoughts of returning home.

I wonder what's taking Azumel so long to send us back to the future. It should have been just as easy as it was to come here. If the real war starts, I don't want to be anywhere near it. It was one thing reading about warfare, but another being in the midst of it!

The feast went by normally though Bobby was sure that everyone else at the table had noticed the scarcity of food. Usually, seafood such as fish and lobster would be present on the menu at such a grand feast, but access to the coast was severely limited as the Toltecs and the Spanish now threatened anyone who left the boundaries. Staple Mayan foods were served first such as maize, squash, beans and chili peppers. Papayas, pineapple, and sweet potatoes were also available. The main dish consisted of tortillas with different types of meats such as turkey, deer and monkey which the hunters had captured several days ago.

The feast continued for the rest of the afternoon. Musicians played traditional Mayan songs on flutes while children danced to the tunes. Bobby and Eli mostly remained in their seats, talking casually with their Mayan friends and enjoying the experience.

After the feast ended, Itzkas hurried to Bobby and Eli who were getting ready to leave. The general had a worried look on his face.

"Come with me. The council is meeting! There are urgent matters to be discussed with the King!"

The three proceeded to the palace while the rest of the Mayans returned to their homes.

"What's the matter, Itzkas?" asked Bobby.

"More disturbing news has come from our allies. The evils along our borders are growing."

They reached the palace entrance and the guards ushered them in. King Topiltzin and the council, along with Chiccan of Lamanal, were sitting with looks of great distress on their faces. Once Bobby and Eli had taken their places, the King spoke.

"Everyone is here. Now let us discuss this new intelligence. Ghanan?"

Ghanan, a senior scout, walked to the center of the floor.

"My Lord, this report just came to me from one of our runners. Several days ago, a large contingent of foreigners landed a little ways south of Nim Li Punit. News of what had happened at Lamanal had spread there so King Chamer was prepared. He sent a couple of scouts but when they did not return, he ordered all women, children and old men to leave for Chich'en Itzá. He and the rest of the men remained to defend the citadel."

"So these foreigners are coming in increasingly larger numbers. And you say they are building settlements, too?"

"Yes, my lord. The other scouts reported that they were cutting down even more trees to build large houses. Some of their men were coming down from the north to trade with them."

The council pondered his words for several minutes until Ghanan broke the silence.

"But that is not the most troubling part."

King Topiltzin looked up.

"What do you mean, Ghanan?"

"While the people of Nim Li Punit were leaving, several of the scouts noticed what appeared to be local men meeting with the foreigners in their homes. The men were laughing and exchanging items with the foreigners. Thinking that this was odd, these scouts hid behind the bushes close to the homes. When they got near enough, they saw that it was the Toltecs."

The council took a deep collective breath. King Topiltzin closed his eyes as if he knew this already.

"How can you be sure?"

"The scouts could tell based on the clothing. Similar news also has come from the other towns. The Toltecs and these foreigners have allied. That is the only meaning."

The King looked up and said, "I have come to the same conclusion. It is as I feared. Our worst enemy and these newcomers have allied."

Turning to the council, he asked, "Now what options do we have?"

For some time no one spoke. Then someone ventured, "Should we flee? It will be a long and arduous journey, but can we withstand the might of this new enemy? Especially the might of their weaponry!"

"Are you crazy, Hunhau?" another prince shouted. "Even if we do flee, these foreigners will continue to come and try to take our land once more. Then should we flee again?" Other princes murmured in agreement.

"I agree with Prince Itzamma," said Chiccan. "The new alliance explains the brazenness of the Toltecs. Our strength will fall if we do nothing. Action must be taken!"

King Topiltzin stood thinking for several minutes.

Then he ordered, "Send out signals to all our allies for as many able men as they can muster!"

Scouts and heralds rushed to carry out those commands. The King turned to the council.

"Let our enemy come marching here! We will fight to the glory of Kukulcan! The fate of our time will be decided at Chich'en Itzá."

Eli turned to Bobby.

"So it has begun."

CHAPTER TWELVE

For the next several weeks, Mayans and their allies traveled to Chich'en Itzá. Five hundred men came from Tikal and Calakmal, the closest cities to Chich'en Itzá. A week later, two hundred men came from Tonina and three hundred and fifty from Bonampak, the cities to the north. The largest contingent of a thousand men had come from Tulum, the sister city of Chich'en Itzá. Lastly, seven hundred men each came from Quirigua and Copan, the border cities to the south. After this, the gates of Chich'en Itzá were closed.

Main temple at Tulum against the Caribbean Sea. Tulum managed to survive about 70 years after the Spanish began occupying Mexico.

"Where are the rest of our warriors?" whispered the people. "At least two thousand more should have come."

"So few are here," said Itzkas.

And yet King Topiltzin was not overly worried.

"We are fine for now. We are still in the midst of the Uayeb. The Toltecs will not attack us now."

Bobby asked Itzkas, "Why would the Toltecs not attack us just because it is festival time?"

Itzkas nodded in acknowledgement.

"True, for the Toltecs are a warlike people. But even they would not dare to attack during the Uayeb festival. The priests have not told you the significance of Uayeb?"

Bobby shook his head.

"The Uayeb are five extra days added to the end of the year. It is a time of prayer and rites of purification because unlucky barriers between the underworld and the real world are opened during this period. We fast to purify our bodies and souls. It is a very important occasion because, like the Tzolkin, it concerns our main god, Kukulcan."

Itzkas paused before adding, "We may fight at any other time, but none of our neighbors, not even the savage Toltecs, conduct warfare during this festival. Remember, our life centers around time. War during this festival is unlucky, and all of us stay away from it."

I hope he is right! thought an alarmed Bobby. *The Mayans are going to be extremely weak if they are fasting.*

But the council was sure that war would not begin until the Uayeb was over.

Two days after the gates were closed, Itzkas came to the brothers' room before they had left for work.

"Come, I have something to show you," he said elatedly. "You will appreciate it later."

They left the room and walked across the plaza under the soft gaze of the morning sun. They hurried past the temples towards a long row of mud huts that were assembled beside the farm fields.

"What's happened, Itzkas?" asked Bobby. The general seemed very happy, something that the brothers had not seen in a long time, not since the troubles began.

"My father, Nurav, is back! He was in the hospital for ages, ever since a Toltec shot him with a poisoned arrow. But by the blessings of Kukulcan, he is alive!"

Bobby knew that the Mayans had extremely advanced medical techniques for their time. He had spent a few days in the hospital himself after sustaining a bad hit to the hand, by an ulama ball, and was amazed by the skills of the priests who practiced medicine.

"Medicine in Mayan culture is a blend of religion and science," they told him. "The priests learn and administer it, that way the blessings of Kukulcan will be with the patient as well."

After the priests completed the hand surgery, they showed Bobby their instruments. "See this blade that we use? It is made of obsidian, because obsidian blades cut cleaner and the patients heal quicker with less scar tissue. This knowledge is what we have acquired over the years and we are proud of it."

Afterwards, they pointed to several dried herbs on a table beside the bed. "Those herbs are very effective too. We use them to alleviate common diseases such as pinta, leishmaniasis and yellow fever. To Mayans, good health is the perfect "balance," while disease and illness create imbalance. That is why, unlike our neighbors who learn war, we spend time learning medicine."

––––––––––––––––––

It's amazing that Itzkas's father still lives at his old age...especially after getting hit by a poisoned arrow, thought Bobby.

"So, he was a soldier for a living?" he asked Itzkas.

"No...he was a farmer like the ones you work with every day. Then one day, many years ago while he was at the border city of Palenque, he was shot with an arrow by the Toltecs. It was in an area unfamiliar to him, by the Usumacinta River. Luckily, he survived just long enough for the priests to save him. When they told me that he was alive...that was the happiest moment of my life," he replied, his voice brimming with emotion.

They stopped when they reached the house. It was a small mud hut with rounded corners, no windows and one door that faced the rising sun.

This was where Itzkas lived? thought Bobby incredulously. It seemed remarkable that the famed scout and general had come from such humble beginnings.

Itzkas knocked on the door and opened it. The three walked in. The floor of the home was made of *sascab,* a foundation of gravel covered with white packed soil. The walls consisted of wood, covered with adobe and then whitened with lime. The roof was circular and was also made of wood tied together to form beams. All in all, the entire house could not have been more than the size of Bobby's bedroom.

"Father?" whispered Itzkas.

What Bobby had taken for a pile of rags shook and looked up. Nurav was a wizened old man with wrinkles all over his face. He had the look of a person who had gone through much in his life, and now just wanted peace and time with his children.

"My boy, why have you come so early? Your brothers live next door and have not even visited yet," he said in a slow, deep voice. Then he added, "Well, you were always the best."

Itzkas smiled. "Father, I just wanted you to meet two of my friends, Bobby and Eli. They were newcomers who came while you were still sick. They have been invaluable to us."

Nurav gazed at the brothers. "Good," he replied. "The Mayans need as much help as possible. Stay with Itzkas; you will learn much for there are not many men like him."

Nurav closed his eyes and fell back into his hammock.

Itzkas said, "Don't worry; an old man needs his sleep."

He covered his father tenderly with a worn, colorful blanket and continued, "After someone marries, it's Mayan tradition for the community to gather and build the new couple's home. When I marry, it will be the same. But even after marrying, it is our custom to keep our parents under the same roof. Sending them off is an insult to everything they have done for us."

Bobby followed Itzkas closely listening to every word. Eli responded questioningly. "Itzkas, your father said that all your brothers live nearby. How come you don't?"

Itzkas replied, "Yes, I would have been farming too for my family is of the lower class. But one day as I was practicing archery, King Topiltzac, our king's father, and his friends galloped past my home. He must have seen me practicing, for the King stopped and asked me what my name was. Then he asked if I would accompany him to the palace to be one of his soldiers. Of course I said yes!" He smiled in remembrance.

"My father was so happy; he wanted one of us to become great... but I owe everything I am to him."

Nurav snored and said something unintelligible under his breath. Itzkas asked the brothers if they would excuse him so that he could spend some more personal time with his dad. The brothers thanked him and left.

Once outside, Eli shook his head. "Itzkas is one of the noblest people I have ever met. Imagine letting our parents stay with us for the rest of our lives," he said in an alarmed tone.

"Yes, but if you think about it, we do owe everything to our parents," replied Bobby.

"I guess..."

The two walked back to get ready for work. Thoughts of Itzkas and his dad were still in their heads.

As the days passed, massive measures were being taken to safeguard the city. Because Chich'en Itzá itself was a citadel, not a fortress, the Mayans began to dig fortifications around the city. Bobby and Eli were involved in the preparation. It was long and tiresome work, for these encirclements had to be built around the entire city as the Mayans did not know from which side the Toltecs and their allies would attack. Defense towers were also being built from which large stones and arrows could be fired.

It was on the second day of this work, when many of the soldiers had left on a patrol, that Azumel came to Bobby and Eli. This was unusual, for the Chief Priest had not spoken to them for a long time. The last time they had met, he had told them that it was proving to be extremely difficult to find a way to send the brothers back to the future. In fact, it was most likely that Bobby and Eli would have to spend the rest of their lives in Chich'en Itzá.

But now Azumel was hurrying along towards the two of them with an excited look on his face.

"Hey Eli! Look who's coming. Seems the old priest, or should I call him chief astronomer, finally has some good news!"

"Yes, I hope so. I've begun to lose confidence in his skills. Did you notice he's been acting oddly lately, especially after the King's declaration of war?" replied Eli.

Bobby shrugged. "He's the King's Chief Priest. He's been under a lot of pressure lately. Especially after what happened last month."

Eli shook his head in agreement. About a month ago, the Toltecs ambushed several Mayan groups and killed a top Mayan general, Harappan. Although ambushes were common nowadays, the bizarre thing was that the attacks occurred at the northern and southern borders simultaneously, just when the Mayans were leaving for

Chich'en Itzá. The Toltecs assaulted the completely defenseless camp and over 500 died, sending a ripple of fear throughout the Mayan cities. King Topiltzin had publicly rebuked Azumel for failing to foresee these attacks, further straining their tenuous relationship. Bobby remembered seeing the high priest walk out of the palace muttering to himself.

As Azumel approached, Bobby noticed something odd. He knew that the Mayans had a strict class system, with the King being the most powerful, followed by the priests, with the workers at the bottom. It was very rare for a chief priest to be in close proximity with the lower classes. But today, Azumel was walking directly toward some very surprised workers, who dropped everything they were doing, looking curiously and with admiration at the priest. Giving the workers a condescending look, Azumel turned his attention to the brothers.

"Bobby, Eli! I have some exciting news for you! My priests have finally discovered how to send you back to the future!"

He smiled, noticing their looks of incredulity.

"I know; it has been years. But one can never be too careful when transporting precious cargo into time."

Eli looked at the priest with an uncertain expression on his face.

"How did you finally get it correct?"

Azumel smiled again.

"It is an extremely complicated process so I cannot properly explain it here. But now come with me! We cannot waste any more time, lest the proper conditions and cosmic alignment disappear! Don't bring any of your belongings with you."

The priest motioned for the boys to follow him and hurried to the temple.

"Looks like they actually know their stuff," said Eli, beaming with enthusiasm. "Brother, we're finally going home."

Bobby smiled and then laughed aloud, along with his brother.

"Wow, do you think Mother will even recognize us? Cause I can't remember how she looked," Eli said excitedly.

"We did miss Mom and Dad all these years, didn't we?" Bobby asked, noticing the joy on Eli's face. Eli was certainly his mother's pet.

"Yeah! I miss her hug so much. If we survived here as well as we did all these years, it is because of her. Remember Bobby—how she used to try to get us involved in so many things at home, and make us handle more and more tasks on our own?" Eli reminisced, his voice betraying him.

Looking at him, Bobby thought, *This is the first time in years Eli has shown any emotion. He has been remarkably strong.* Brotherly warmth slowly engulfed him.

"Come here, Eli," Bobby said, extending his arms.

The brothers hugged each other. Bobby thought of the days back home when they used to roughhouse with each other. Amazingly, they were such a good team here in this strange Mayan world. After everything they had gone through together, Bobby could not understand how they could ever have fought over such petty things as which channel to watch on TV, who got to play the Wii, and who got access to the cookie box first.

"Grow up—you cannot achieve great things if you focus on petty issues," their mom would always say, trying to interject and stop an all-out fight. Well, they certainly had grown up now.

"Dad too...working hard to provide for our needs."

Momentarily lost in blissfulness, the pair headed to the temple. They were finally going home. Or so they thought.

Chapter Thirteen

Once they entered the temple, Azumel motioned for them to follow him down a narrow corridor. Bobby and Eli looked at each other.

"We never came this way," remarked Bobby.

"Yes, but now we are going via a more secure route for the launch. Do not worry; I know what I am doing," replied Azumel.

The trio walked for several minutes before they reached a back doorway, and entered a dark alley that was behind the city.

"Good. They should be here any moment now," muttered the old priest to himself, rubbing his palms.

The brothers looked at the high priest quizzically.

"Where is everyone? Where are we, Azumel?" asked Bobby.

Disregarding the question, Azumel pointed to a spot close to him.

"You two must come closer! I need to secure both of you together, so you can be transported as one. That will reduce the risk," He moved Eli towards Bobby, with Eli's back touching Bobby's. Then he took a long red cloth, and bound their hands and legs so tightly that they could scarcely move.

Suddenly, in such a swift motion that it belied his age, Azumel secured red opaque cloths around Bobby's and Eli's eyes.

"What are you doing, Azumel?" yelled out Bobby.

Azumel did not respond and continued binding the boys tighter. Bobby could feel Eli grappling with the bands around his face and arms, but the old priest had made sure the bands were tight.

"Let go!" shouted Eli.

"I cannot. My master has forbidden me to, under punishment of death," said Azumel in a low voice.

"What are you talking about?" demanded Bobby.

Suddenly a cloth fell over the brothers' faces and instant darkness took over.

Blackness covered Bobby and Eli for a long time. After a while, Bobby heard horses and what seemed to be a chariot approaching. *Where did they come from? Mayans don't have horses!*

"Everything went fine, Metzametel?" asked Azumel anxiously.

"Yes," replied a man with an extremely deep voice, like a lion's growl. "The side gate was open, as you said, and the sentries dead."

Bobby could hear metal clanking as Metzametel and his men climbed off their horses.

"These are the correct people, Azumel? I would hate to think what King Hurukan would do to you if the wrong Mayans were captured."

"Yes, yes, they are the ones," said Azumel restlessly. "Quick, we do not have much time. King Topiltzin and the rest of the men will come back soon."

Hearing the name of Hurukan being mentioned, Bobby now knew that they were being captured by the Toltecs. His heart seemed to stop breathing, and he felt a shiver in his spine. The brothers were forced onto a chariot along with a Toltec as the guide. The other men got on their horses and began galloping in the direction they had come from. Bobby thought worriedly— *What's going on? Everything is happening so fast.*

They kept riding this way for what seemed like hours.

All along, they could hear Azumel slowly humming under his breath. Bobby and Eli listened in anger. Finally, the men halted their horses and then loosened the ropes around the brothers' legs so that the two could walk. Hours of forced riding with hands and legs tied had made the brothers extremely stiff, and they fell to the ground immediately. Azumel jabbed them both hard with something pointed. "Get up, xiipals!"

Unsteadily, the brothers slowly managed to stand up. Bobby could hear the sound of birds and leaves fluttering in the wind. He could sense he was in a forest.

"I must go to lead my men," said Metzametel. Leaning closer to the high priest, so that Bobby could only catch pieces of what was being said, Metzametel whispered to Azumel.

"Lock securely...use bronze rod...Hurukan angry." Azumel said something in return and Metzametel and his men galloped away.

Azumel pushed the brothers forward, making them walk. Bobby and Eli tried to talk to him, but were silenced with sharp jabs to their backs. After a few minutes, Bobby heard Azumel knocking on a door. A squeaking sound followed, signaling an old door being opened. They heard someone come out and walk towards them.

"Here are the prisoners," said Azumel in a hurried tone. The high priest uncovered their faces, as if proving that he was handing over the right people.

The sudden brightness of the sun blinded Bobby's eyes. He shut them tightly, and then opened them after a few seconds. A stout man stood before him, sword in hand. Bobby could tell he was a Toltec warrior based on his militaristic attire. He began wrestling with the ropes that were still around his arms.

"Don't do anything stupid," said Azumel, pointing towards the gun in his hand. The Toltec nodded to Azumel. Taking out a bronze rod from his pocket, Azumel walked quickly into the building.

The Toltec grabbed them with abnormal strength and pushed them towards the stone building. It was an old and sinister looking barracks. Rows of human skulls and heads lined up the outer wall. Displayed prominently on the wall was a head; it looked uncomfortably familiar: it did not have a ear. Bobby remembered Harappan, the one—eared general.

The forest's trees nearly concealed the building, making it hard for an outsider to spot. The Toltec guard shoved the brothers in, and then led them down to a cell. It was cold, dark, and smelled of decaying flesh. Making sure that both their hands were still secure, he said in a harsh voice, "You will remain here until King Hurukan wishes to see you." He slammed the door shut. The sound of his boots echoed as he left.

Silence and darkness met the brothers. Their only comfort was each other.

"I can't believe Azumel was a traitor!" whispered Eli.

"Me neither...remember how nervous he was when King Topiltzin declared war? It makes sense now. He never wanted to send us to the future...he was just waiting for a chance to turn us over to the Toltecs," replied Bobby. He had reached that conclusion during the kidnapping.

Tired, they sat thinking about what awaited them. Several hours seemed to pass, with only the occasional sound of crickets chirping in the distance.

When the brothers were drifting away into sleep, they sensed someone shaking them. Two new Toltec soldiers were bending over them, untying the ropes around their legs. The brothers were pushed roughly back outside where the soft breeze of the night greeted them.

Bobby and Eli were thrust on the ground. When they looked up, what they saw scared them. An enormous man with knives tucked all around his body, and a huge red sword in one hand, stood with his legs wide apart, staring at them. His face was hardened by several long scars that ran along his forehead. Behind him stood numerous other fierce looking Toltecs.

"Wh—who are you?" asked Bobby, shaken.

"I am Hurukan, King of the Toltecs. I believe you two are very valuable to me," replied the king.

"What?" Eli managed to say.

"You are from the future. So, I asked my reliable spy, Azumel, to bring you here. You will tell me the future," said King Hurukan. "Then I will use it as I wish."

Noticing the looks of fear on the brothers' faces, the Toltec king laughed aloud and commented, "You two should be happy. After all, you are going to be much luckier than your Mayan friends."

A messenger appeared from the forest.

"My lord, the Spanish are here. We will attack when you give the command."

Bobby could not believe his ears and he lost all of his earlier apprehension.

"What do you mean "attack"? It is the festival of Uayeb! There is a time of peace until the festival is over."

Hurukan snorted.

"Yes, my people followed those silly rules before, too. But a new people from the east have landed on our shores."

King Hurukan had an intense look in his eyes as he described his meetings with the men from the east.

"They showed me that I am free to do whatever I wish. They taught me that there is no such thing as right or wrong, there are only the strong and those too weak to fight them. Winner takes all!"

He paused, his face set.

"Now with their help, nothing can stop the Toltecs!"

Eli tugged at his ropes, his cheeks red with emotion.

"You are despicable. Can you not at least fight fairly? You know that the Mayans will be weak physically during the Uayeb fasting."

"The Mayans are fools and they deserve to die," Hurukan replied curtly. "They spend their time gazing at the stars, while we perfect the art of war."

The other Toltecs snickered.

"Besides, even in a fair fight, the Mayans would still be obliterated. For my new allies have weapons that can destroy many men with one shot. Weapons that the Mayans cannot even dream about."

Eli continued straining against the ropes about his arms, an angry, wretched look on his face. In a last-ditch attempt to change the Toltec leader's mind, he cried out, "If you attack, then we will not tell you anything about the future!"

King Hurukan gestured at his dagger. "There are other ways to make you talk."

He addressed the guards.

"Throw them back in the dungeon. I will deal with them again once we are finished."

The Toltec soldiers grabbed the struggling brothers and dragged them with difficulty back into the dark barracks' cell, closing the entrance.

The King turned to the rest of the Toltecs. "Get ready, my Toltec brothers. Tonight we attack!"

Bobby could not help but think about what the Mayans were doing right now. They were probably praying and fasting piously, completely unaware of the events on the horizon.

Once again the brothers waited in darkness.

Chapter Fourteen

"Eli, you okay?" asked Bobby.

"Yes, I'm fine. So much for going back home," replied Eli sadly.

Bobby tried to push against the barred door, but it did not budge.

Suddenly, he heard a knock on top of the cell.

"Shhh..." Bobby motioned to Eli.

The boys held their breath and listened. The knock came again, this time more pronounced.

"Who's there?" called Bobby softly.

After a few moments, a familiar voice replied in an urgent tone.

"It's me, Itzkas. I tried to follow after Azumel kidnapped you, but some Toltecs found me. Kukulcan gave me strength to overpower them, but not before I discovered that you two were in a cell here."

"Itzkas! The Toltecs are going to attack!" Eli cried out. At this point the brothers were more worried about the Mayans than their own fate.

"I heard everything. I just hope that we are prepared," replied Itzkas. He reached for his bag and took out a small metal stick.

"Can you get us out of here?" whispered Eli.

"Yes. This is a special stick which has gotten me out of several dungeons in my time," smiled Itzkas. He took out the silver rod and touched the lock of the dungeon cell, while in a low voice reciting incantations under his breath. After several long moments, the cell door opened and Bobby and Eli climbed out.

"Praise Kukulcan," hailed Itzkas. The three ran out to the corridor.

Two unconscious Toltec guards lay on the ground; the trio quickly stripped them of their weapons.

"My work," said Itzkas, "My training taught me the skills of stealth warfare at an early age. Let's get out of here before more Toltecs arrive."

They departed the barracks and felt the brisk night air. A bright moon greeted them and under its soothing light they saw hundreds of soldiers making their way down a dirt road at a distance.

"Soldiers. Quick, hide!" commanded Itzkas, "We'll wait for a smaller group."

The boys knelt down behind several bushes. After some moments, they noticed a small patrol of three Toltecs upon horses approaching. Itzkas turned towards the brothers. "You wait here. I will get those horses. Just make sure that no soldier catches sight of you."

He quickly slipped away, his feet quietly trampling the leaves on the ground.

"He'll be okay," said Bobby, reassuring himself as well as Eli. "King Topiltzin didn't make him a general for nothing."

"Hopefully. But we don't know if the Mayans can withstand the full Toltec might," said Eli, despairingly. "And how on earth are we getting home in this mess?"

Bobby peered at the moon. Returning seemed more distant than ever.

"If we can't make it back, then we're going to stay here and fight. The Mayans treated us as one of them."

With a firm resolve on his face, Eli shook his head in agreement. Bobby was sure that his younger brother was ready to give his all for the generous people who took care of them for so long.

They waited for quite a while, listening to the rhythm of soldiers marching in the distance.

Suddenly Eli whispered, "Look Bobby! Someone's coming." Bobby looked to the east, and slowly he could decipher Itzkas, his stout muscular form steadily making its way towards the boys with several horses at his heels.

"Yes!" uttered Bobby, under his breath.

Itzkas came to a stop beside the boys and said, "Quickly! Hurukan and his men are fast marching towards Chich'en Itzá. Get on these horses; they are easy to ride." The boys leapt onto their respective horses and galloped off through the woods.

"You okay?" asked Eli.

"Yes," said Bobby. To the west, under the glow of the moon, he could see the Toltec soldiers, in long lines, snaking towards Chich'en Itzá. He guessed that the battle would begin in a day's time, but still too quick for the Mayans to prepare. Taking the route through the woods was much faster, according to Itzkas, and no one would see them. In the distance, Bobby could hear the trumpeting of the enemy soldiers and he prayed that King Topiltzin would be ready for the attack. The three of them galloped hard for several more hours through the thick forest, until they reached the Vigia River.

Stopping his horse, Itzkas looked at the brothers and said, "Once we pass this river, there is no turning back. Do you understand?" Bobby and Eli nodded solemnly. Itzkas gazed up at the moon.

"Only Kukulcan knows our fate now."

CHAPTER FIFTEEN

"Hurry up, hurry up!" cried Hurukan.

The Toltec king barked at his second-in-command, "Metzametel, can't you make these men move any faster? At this rate, Topiltzin will have time to order all his troops out. We must capture them by surprise if we want to obliterate them."

Metzametel bowed and galloped toward the troops. Hurukan looked in the direction of Chich'en Itzá.

But even if Topiltzin mobilizes all his troops, they stand no chance. The mighty Toltecs have come!

A Spanish officer on horseback trotted to his side.

King Hurukan asked, "San Fernando, where are your men?"

"My men are traveling in small contingents with your troops. We have brought much artillery for this operation. The full might of Spain will be on display tonight," the Spaniard replied, his chin raised in confidence.

King Hurukan smiled, pleased.

———————————

Not far away from the Toltec troops, Itzkas, Bobby, Eli and King Topiltzin overlooked the preparations for the battle. Hundreds of Mayan soldiers were making their way towards the battlefield.

"Are you sure about what you saw?" asked King Topiltzin.

"Yes," replied Itzkas. "There were at least 10,000 Toltecs marching under Hurukan. But that's not the worst of it. There were also some of the Spaniards marching alongside the Toltecs. They have brought many of their weapons with them."

King Topiltzin thrust his sword into the ground with force, displaying his anger.

"I cannot believe I trusted that traitor Azumel for so long. How could he do this, under the tutelage of Kukulcan?"

"Power and wealth! They made him greedy. He was promised his own kingdom," Itzkas answered, his voice deep with a combination of anger, resentment and sadness.

"We cannot ponder on the past now," King Topiltzin replied, pulling himself together, "We have to put our full focus on the enemy. If Kukulcan truly wants the Mayan race to live on, then he will deliver victory in our favor. If he has other plans, so be it. We will give this fight our all!" His voice boomed with determination.

"I have told our priests about the impending urgent situation. They were caught by surprise because we have never battled during the Uayeb, but they have hurriedly begun their religious rites," said Itzkas.

The king moved forward, facing the rising sun. "May the grace of Kukulcan be with us!"

Chapter Sixteen

"Move up, move up! Infantry in front, archers in back. Move up, move up!"

Thousands of men were waiting on the Chiapas Highlands. They had been gathering throughout the hours of that long day. The Puuc hills could be seen at a distance before the sea, looming like guardians of a New World. The enemy waited just two miles across the field. Last-minute decisions and human sacrifices were being made to request the support of Kukulcan on the Mayan side. As king, Topiltzin had to make sure his men were ready for battle.

The Spanish were what caused the king private concern; he had heard of great battles that they had fought, with weaponry unfamiliar to his generals.

However, with a voice that echoed resilience and confidence, the king addressed his lieutenants, "Chiccan, take your men up the western side. Try to cover the flank with cavalry, and then shoot the enemy down with your archers. Kukulcan be with you."

In reply, Chiccan swore to the King. "My lord, I will fight to my last breath for the glory of Lamanal and the Mayans." He walked away.

King Topiltzin then commanded the second general. "Hunhau, take your spearmen up the front and try to hold the enemy as long as you can, until Chiccan covers the flank. Do not let the Spanish overtake you. Kukulcan be with you." Hunhau bowed and rushed off.

Once he had finished giving orders to all of his generals, King Topiltzin turned towards Itzkas. He raised his head slightly, and closing his eyes as if what he was about to say was painful, the King took a deep breath and continued, "Itzkas, take Bobby and Eli with you back to the temple. I want the three of you to go back to the future."

Bobby had never heard the king speak this way before.

After taking in the implication of what he had heard, Itzkas began protesting loudly, "My lord, I am your general! I can't go back when everyone else—"

King Topiltzin cut him off.

"You are my most trusted general, Itzkas. Right now you are the only man I can trust." He pointed out at the growing black expanse that was moving towards Chich'en Itzá.

"See that, my friend? That is what the Mayans have to fight this day. We are outranked badly in number and in weaponry. Our people's future looks dire."

Over their stay, Bobby had not seen Itzkas' face look so troubled and pained. Bobby could tell that he wanted to fight until his last breath for the king and the kingdom he so dearly loved.

"As your last duty, I want you to go into the future with these men. Thanks to Kukulcan there is a full moon tonight, favorable for time travel. Then, when you are in the future, I want you to make sure that the Mayans are remembered for their achievements. Remembered for their place in history as a source of knowledge and wisdom for future generations."

Itzkas walked slowly and knelt in front of his king, with tears glistening in his eyes.

The King looked silently at the far horizon and the structures built by his ancestors, against the backdrop of a blood red sky painted by a setting sun. With a steady, distant gaze, he said in a calm voice:

"Remember our alphabet, our mathematics, our medicine."

"Remember our great strides in astronomy! The galaxy, the solar year, the solstices and equinoxes!"

"Remember the famous structures we built!"

"Remember the knowledge we captured on stelae and the books we authored and shared with allies!"

"Remember how we fought and still fight so hard to maintain peace!"

"Lastly, remember Chich'en Itzá and its glories so that your descendants will know what we left on this earth." His voice grew more passionate with each phrase.

"Our legacy should remain preserved for generations to come. Do this, as my final command to you, and you can rest in peace with your honor intact!"

Itzkas was still kneeling before the king, with his head down and palms folded together as a tribute to the man he deeply admired. The mighty general could not break open his voice, and was fighting back tears.

Bobby looked at Itzkas and the king. He walked forward and knelt next to Itzkas, and bowed his head. Then, with equal passion, he replied,

"Don't worry, my lord. The Mayans will be remembered forever. We'll make sure of it."

Eli nodded fervently in agreement.

Itzkas touched the King's hands, and quietly said, "My lord! May the strength of Kukulcan be with you."

The King touched his foremost general's head.

"And with you."

Suddenly, trumpets began once again blaring in the distance. Shouts could be heard along with cries of agony moments later.

The Battle of Chichen Itza

King Topiltzin turned towards the battlefield.

"Farewell, my friends! Remember our ancestors! Remember Chich'en Itzá! Remember the Mayans!"

The trio looked on until the King disappeared into the far distance and could be seen no more.

Chapter Seventeen

The three moved stealthily through the city with Itzkas leading the way making sure that no enemy was hiding, waiting to attack. Bobby looked at the Temple of the Warriors and the Temple of the Tables as they walked past them. Strangely, even after all the recent events, a part of him wanted to remain in this strange, exotic place. After several more moments of thought, he realized that a part of him had become Mayan. This place, no matter what would happen, would always remain in his heart.

They had just passed the towering Temple of Kukulcan. He remembered how when they had first arrived here, he and Eli had been subjected to the most rigorous religious test. Luckily, they had come out clean, but he still remembered the stress of that moment.

Now Bobby could just make out the smaller North Temple and the great ball court where he, Eli and the other Mayan youths had so often played Ulama. Hastily, they walked up the steps until they reached the hallway where less than 24 hours ago, Azumel had tricked them into captivity.

"Quick! Into the main chamber," said Itzkas.

They made their way into the large room lighted with torches. A few of the strange religious tools and artifacts still remained, with most being taken to help the war effort. Itzkas busied himself by shuffling through the items, looking for something specific.

"Itzkas, do you know what you're doing?" Eli asked anxiously.

"Yes. I secretly asked some of the priests how to send you two back, just in case we ever were in a situation like this. They said that a gold circular instrument with inscriptions on it; and a full moon were needed for the transfer."

Eli shouted out, "A full moon! We've had so many of those! We could have been out of here so long ago!"

Itzkas found the tool and turned back to Eli.

"Yes, but you have to remember that Azumel was a traitor. He purposefully kept this information from everybody, and provided the other priests false data about your birth. When I gave them the accurate data, the priests were able to determine the correct plan."

Itzkas picked up the gold circle-shaped item that resembled a full moon. He motioned for Bobby and Eli to follow him outside. But at the moment when they turned to leave, they saw that the path to the door was blocked by a dark shadow.

It was Azumel!

The old priest had never looked so angry. A vein was pulsing in his neck and his face was covered with what seemed like scabs. He had rid himself of his priestly clothes and now was dressed in Toltec war attire, with a dagger hanging at his belt.

"King Hurukan should have killed you scum when he had the chance. I knew you two were wily enough to escape."

"What happened to your face?" asked Bobby.

"Punishment for your escape!" growled Azumel.

"Well, thank whoever did it. You look better this way," added Eli angrily.

But Itzkas looked wary.

"Quick! We have to get out of here before any more of the Toltecs arrive!" He looked at Azumel, "Get out of the way, old man. Kukulcan will decide your fate. I don't even want to see your face! You have done enough harm already."

Azumel laughed.

"Yes. And I'm about to do some more."

With a move so fast that there was no time to react, the former priest and Mayan took out a gun and fired a single bullet at Itzkas.

"NO!" yelled Bobby and Eli.

Azumel replied evenly, "One of the benefits of fighting with the Spanish."

Itzkas leaned forward and then slowly and gracefully fell to the ground. His eyes were still open.

Azumel looked down at his former colleague with no emotion in his eyes.

"Good. Now he is gone." He glanced up.

"You are next!"

In a last attempt to save themselves, Bobby cried out, "But your king needs us! We can tell him the future. What will he say when he finds out we're dead?"

Azumel laughed again. It sounded like a discordant cricket croaking and was painful to hear.

"Then you'll have died in a little accident. Unfortunately for you, the Toltecs do not care about a couple of Mayans dying here and there. As for King Hurukan...well he can conquer the entire world with the aid of the Spanish. So your help is not needed anymore."

Bobby replied, "Fool! Do you honestly trust the Spanish? They will destroy you once they have finished with the Mayans."

Azumel stroked the tip of his gun with one of his long bony fingers.

"Be that as it may, at least I will have the pleasure of killing you." The priest pointed the gun straight at Bobby.

"The older one first."

Bobby closed his eyes for the end of the greatest adventure of his life.

But he felt nothing.

He opened his eyes.

Instead of a bullet coming at him, a dagger was protruding from Azumel's chest. The old priest had a look of shock in his eyes, before falling to the ground as the gun went off with a loud bang. Bobby glanced down and saw Itzkas smiling. Blood was all over his chest but the good general had an expression of peace in his eyes.

Bobby and Eli ran and knelt before him.

Itzkas closed and opened his eyes as he tried to fight off the darkness.

"Remember what King Topiltzin said. Or else our sacrifice would be for nothing."

"We will never forget! Itzkas--We are not going to leave you behind. You will come with us. Remember–you made sure we were strong!" Bobby kept talking frantically, as if to keep Itzkas awake.

"Itzkas--Don't close your eyes--be with us." choked Eli.

Itzkas smiled once more before saying heavily, "No--this is where I belong. This is Kukulcan's wish. Now go quickly! I fear that the Toltecs will breach the citadel soon! Once you reach the main temple, take the gold tool out, trace the inscription, and wait for the full moon to cover you in its light. Then by the will of Kukulcan, you will go back."

Bobby grabbed the gold tool and with Eli raced toward the door.

"Wait!" cried out Itzkas. He tried to move from the floor but the pain was too much and he fell backwards. The brothers ran back to him.

Itzkas reached into his knapsack and took out a book.

"This book contains all of our history and achievements since the beginning of our time. Use it well. I have a feeling that none of the other thousands of recordings will survive." His voice trailed off in sadness.

Bobby took the book from Itzkas's shaking hands, and held it for a moment, before carefully concealing it in his pocket.

With one last look at Itzkas, the two sprinted down the hallway. Once outside, they came to the Temple of Kukulcan, the largest building and most magnificent temple in the city. The full moon was almost directly over it, and its light was almost equally displayed on all sides of the building.

"Quick, Eli," said Bobby. "It's almost midnight!"

The boys stood where they thought the beam of silver light would fall at the twelfth hour. They grasped the gold half-circle, tracing the inscription, and closed their eyes. In the distance they could hear shouts and the sound of metal against metal. But they tried to clear all this from their minds, to focus on the task ahead of them.

Then they sensed it.

It felt familiar, déjà vu. The silver moonlight fell on the brothers perfectly and they began experiencing the tingling sensation that they had felt all those years ago. But this time they were not afraid, for they knew what was going to happen. Bobby pressed his hand tightly against the Mayan book in his pocket. He knew that no matter what happened to Eli and him, the real treasure that needed to be transported out was this book. Feeling it safely tucked in his pocket made him smile. Eli too looked at him with a smile, and at that very moment, the shine of the moon turned into a majestic winding serpent, and engulfed both of them back into the darkness.

About the Author

Nick Cherukuri is a high school student living in Cranbury, New Jersey. In his spare time, he likes to play golf, read, and catch up on his favorite shows. Currently, he is working on another adventure of Bobby and Eli, this one based on an ancient civilization in India.